I0562866

THE AUTHOR'S WIFE VS. THE GIANT ROBOT

and other stories

ADAM-TROY CASTRO

TABLE OF CONTENTS

AN INTRODUCTION: IN THIS CORNER...

Folks, this is just a representative collection of my work.

The stories were chosen because I believe them to be especially good ones. I note that while I write science fiction, fantasy, and horror, I recall the hue and cry when my last couple of collections accented the horror and therefore incurred the wrath of readers who upon encountering even one dark work by me, made impassioned declarations about never reading anything I ever wrote, anymore. Therefore I elected to mostly avoid the deep-cut carnage, this time.

I say, "mostly."

If you are horror-averse, avoid the stories "The Hour in Between" and "Big Stupe and the Buried Big Glowing Booger," which are violent and bloody. I think they're damned good stories and that is why I included them – especially "Hour," which I believe to be among my career heights -- but I do not want readers to go there without warning. They are the only two I will make this warning about.

"Rotten Little Town: An Oral History (Abridged)" was published in a horror magazine, but its carnage is at a remove, mostly implied, and in tone could have gone to a mystery magazine just as easily.

"Monkey Trap" and "The Old Horror Writer" were also published in horror magazines, but are largely mild enough for popular consumption.

Basically, the first half of this little volume is lighter on you than the last half.

Of that first half: "Judi" was my first written response to the untimely and deeply unfair demise of the love of my life; "The Author's Wife Vs. The Giant Robot" was written while she was alive and features her as an on-stage character, accurately reporting her reaction to the narrative during her test-read; "Eros Pratfalled: Or, Adrift in Time And Space with Lasagna and Mary Steenburgen," is a love story, as is "The Time Traveler's Advice to the Lovelorn," a basically one-joke story that I think delivered it well; and "The Thing About Shapes to Come" is a parable about motherhood; and "Many Happy Returns" is just a romp, fine even if some readers did not quite get the physical-comedy ending.

Lots of stuff there, for the folks who demand insulation from my darker offerings, and among those latter only two I recommend for reader discretion.

Even those those two are really really good.

Okay?

Enjoy.

Adam-Troy Castro

JUDI

She sank to the ground on a world without name.

We were far from home, farther than we had ever gone, maybe farther than anyone had ever gone. It was so far away, or at least so strange for some undefinable local cause, that we could have filled volumes with all the alterations in the way things worked; in the ways that light worked, in the way that time worked, in the way that mass worked. We spoke of bringing back word to the learned of my world and hers. We talked of making our names.

We were taking a stroll not far from our ship when she sat down and died.

I remember only that last look she gave me. It was not horror. It was not joy. It was not reassurance, and oh, how I wish it was. It was not even the look I had come to treasure and that I thought I would always have, love. It was astonishment. It was as if she had seen something that I had not, something that rendered all persistence at life futile.

She sat down and she was gone, in a place where a white plain met a black sky.

I could not stay with her and I could not take her with me, not in any way that mattered.

So I returned to the ship and set a course for home, knowing that it too was no longer there, not if she could not be part of it.

I left that white world behind, never to speak of it again.

I did not navigate. The ship had a course to follow. It might or not be the right direction, but with her gone there was no itinerary, no purpose in going anywhere at all. It was just movement. The trip out had been filled with possibility. The trip back was only negation. I slept when I could. I woke when I had to. I ate because my body demanded it. I found no pleasure, or flavor. I suspected that I never would again.

Once, I ordered the hull to go transparent because I yearned to see the stars. I didn't know the coordinates when I did, and did not bother to record them. It was a place like so many other places, between systems, far from any place where humanity or the creatures who rival humanity, breathe air and live what lives creation sees fit to give them. There were countless bright specks of light, pinpricks in the cold and the dark, and I knew that once upon a time in the recent past she and I would have stood here together, enthralled, thinking of all those worlds, and all the wonders they held within their bubbles of atmosphere; all those civilizations, those millennia of history, those unsuspected creatures and those treasures in coin unknown to us; and once we would have drawn closer, comforting each other with gentle hopeful lies of how we would live to see them all. The wonder I would have felt, not so long ago, was gone. I was not a creature of the stars, now. I was rather a creature of the vacuum now, of the void that could not support a life worth living.

I made the hull opaque again and restored full speed.

I let the ship make all the decisions. My only command was that it leave her behind.

I did not pay attention to where it took me.

It retraced our trip out.

It passed the ten thousand worlds that made up human space.

It passed the worlds that had names.

It passed the worlds that had been mapped but had not been visited.

It passed the worlds that were home to others, who may have looked up and wondered about the purpose and destination of this one particular speck of light, passing through the darkness.

It passed the worlds ruined by past cataclysms.

It passed through regions where there were no worlds.

It passed through stark emptiness.

By that time I had long since lost even academic curiosity about the details, no interest in enduring the pointless voyage, and so put myself to sleep for as long as I could, suppressing dreams.

It was not life.

It was only the oblivion I wanted.

I do not know how long I slept. Centuries. Millennia. Eons. The ship could keep me alive. It just could not make what life it forced into me worth living. This was not a problem because I refused to let the details in.

I could have killed myself. But it was not what I wanted. There is a difference between wanting to die and not having a reason to live. I did not want to pilot the ship into some raging sun, and for its fires to reduce me to my component atoms. That was not me. But I did not want to make planetfall, did not want to see another face, whether human or creature that had different features I might not recognize as a face. I did want this to be over. But I would not exert the effort to finish it.

Then the alarm woke me.

The ship told me that it had found a place to land and that I had to go outside.

I rose and put on my suit and stepped out onto the surface of another alien world, one not at all special. The stars in its sky fit no recognizable patterns, not to these human eyes; maybe the ship could have used them to navigate back to some world where people still congregated, but as the dust crunched beneath my boots I preferred to think that I had traveled beyond its ability to map, or been in flight so long that I was now the last human being, anywhere; as alone in the universe in fact as I had felt since the moment since she first sank to the chalky dust.

It was a lifeless and airless world, with nothing of note between me and the horizon. There was nothing to see here and would not be, no matter how far I marched, how carefully I mapped. It was just a cold and silent rock, like the one I had in my chest. It was an unimaginable distance from the place where she had died; one even farther away from familiar places than that lonely world, farther away than we had ever gone, and possibly further away than anyone had ever gone. And yet there was nothing at all exotic about it. It was just a place, like any other place.

I could not think of any reason why my ship would have brought me here, let alone urge me to stand on this earth, beneath these pitiless stars.

I just wanted to break, the irrevocable kind of break, that admitted no possibility of unwanted repair.

And that's when I knew that it had been useless to flee.

There was nowhere I could go, anywhere, that could be far enough to leave her behind.

THE AUTHOR'S WIFE
vs. THE GIANT ROBOT

The year I turned five, my father got taken out by a giant robot.

I was present and I took it very personally. You honestly don't expect that kind of thing when you're a kid, not even if you've seen the giant robot from a distance every day of your life and have been taught what random carnage the giant robot got up to.

I had grown to that tender age knowing that the giant robot killed people at the rate of one a day, but this was a story I took only as seriously as those other childhood myths, Santa Claus and the Tooth Fairy, both of which I had already rejected as short on evidence. I couldn't say that about the giant robot. It undeniably existed, in the same way I knew that there were bad people from whom, for some reason, I should not accept candy. I had been given a strategy to avoid those people: don't take candy. I had not been given a strategy for avoiding death by giant robot. There was no strategy. The robot killed who it wanted to.

The robot was four thousand feet tall. It had the approximate contours of a naked man, stylized, with the fortunate exception of genitalia. Our city had never been forced to live in proximity with its dangling junk. It stood with its feet planted a comfortable distance apart, each in a lot which, absent the capacity for further development, was now ground zero for selfie takers. The two parks were several blocks apart and there was an entire neighborhood between them, home to small businesses and the apartments of people who didn't mind living in the shadow under the robot's sexless crotch. The two legs, purple and gleaming, joined in the hips that the leviathan's fists were also planted on, as it stood akimbo in frank ownership of all it surveyed. It had a chest of streamlined musculature, a squat neck, and a face devoid of nose or personality that nevertheless possessed shallow indentations where the eyes and mouth should have been.

Over the years people had tried to give the giant robot names adequate to communicate its majesty. In a religious era, people had called it Jehovah, or the Angel of Death. In a more poetic one, some had dubbed it Ozymandias. When the Academy Awards were new some jokers had said it was just the first Oscar. But all those nicknames had faded and for seventy years now the names had devolved to utility. It was the Giant Robot. Sometimes the Giant Freaking Robot. Sometimes That Fucking Giant Robot. But ultimately, the giant robot.

I knew it was famous for killing one person a day. But until that day I never imagined that could have included any of us. My father was a municipal bus driver, my mother a teaching assistant. We lived two flights up from a village grocery. We were not the kind of people giant robots ever bothered. We were far from the center of town, where the giant stood, and well out of what we imagined to be the giant robot's reach; it mostly went for people within a three-mile radius of where it had planted itself. My father had taken me to see it once, because every kid wants to see the giant robot close up. I only barely remember the day. I must have pronounced it awesome.

A stranger took a photo of my father and I about a block from the giant robot's big toe. I am sitting on my dad's shoulders, making the kind of face a child my age would just automatically use as a default for ferocity. You can see a few dozen other tourists, having a great time as they took their photos in front of the giant robot. Nobody looks particularly scared, even though the deal with the giant robot was the one random person it chose to crush every single day. It was a big city and the odds were always against the designated victim being you or anyone you knew, a small price for the boon it had been for the local economy, both as a tourist site and as an active convenience, given that it gave off enough surplus electricity to spare the city any need for a paycheck-draining power plant. This was a good thing, overall. Most cities didn't get free power from giant robots. We were ahead of the deal.

This of course became harder for me to rationalize when I was five and my father became the designated crushee. It wasn't a good day.

You need to understand that the robot didn't crush my dad by stepping on him. It had been standing in the same spot since my grandfather was a boy, a good thing since it was so heavy it could not have traveled any great distance on foot without causing an earthquake with every step.

Nor did it crush my dad with its gigantic fists; that heroic stance it had affected from the moment of its arrival had also never altered, not by so much as a twitch. But once a day, at about 3:00 in the afternoon, a long flexible coil emerged from a sliding panel in its chest, whipped across a distance that could cover the entire metropolitan area, and sought out the one person it had selected for execution. It did not matter where that one person was. He or she could be at work, or at home, or traveling across town in a taxi, or underground on a subway, or in the prison complex along the river. The robot simply declared a name on the message board mounted on its forehead, and nailed whoever it was with that coil, any attempt at escape futile, not that anybody had ever experienced enough advance warning to try.

For us, it was a Saturday and I was at home with my Dad, playing some board game involving a trio of mice racing around a circular board trying to stay ahead of a cat. My mother had gone to the store for a minute and I remember my father really getting into the game, saying things like, "Squeak! Squeak!" to add immediacy to the adventures of the mice, or, "Oh no, here he comes," whenever the big rubber squeak-toy that represented the cat scurried closer to our tokens, threatening an early end to the game. I remember doing what a five-year-old does, laughing like an idiot. Then the window shattered and something I interpreted as a snake shot across our living room to the coffee table where the two of us were playing our game, wrapped itself around my dad's head and constricted with unimaginable force.

Not every means the robot uses for its daily sacrifice involves a big mess; sometimes it uses gas, sometimes lethal injections, sometimes electric shock. Sometimes the victims die so peacefully that doctors can't even determine the precise source of death. Head-crushing, I've learned, is fairly rare, not that it functioned as much of a consolation. I remember a sound like a balloon popping, only more liquid, and then all of a sudden the snaky thing was gone and the walls were dripping. I heard neighbors shouting in the hallway. Everything was different after that, but then again, it was different every day, for somebody.

• • • •

There is at this point an objection from the Author's Wife.

The Author is not an abstraction meant to stand in for all human beings of his class, except, of course, insofar as he does. He is a specific person. He is, in fact, this author, the one who wrote that sentence, and this one. Also this sentence fragment. And this one. Because he is a specific person, so is his wife, and therefore we need not go into any pedantic objections to the effect that not all authors are men, or have wives. Were he an abstraction those objections would be pointed but accurate. However, he is me. And the Author's Wife is mine.

The Author's Wife:	Who built the robot?
The Author:	I'm not going to worry about that.
The Author's Wife:	I mean, is it from space?
The Author:	I don't know.
The Author's Wife:	This isn't an alien thing?
The Author:	I'm not going to say.
The Author's Wife:	No mad scientist or anything?
The Author:	No.
The Author's Wife:	How did it get there?
The Author:	That's also outside the scope of the story.
The Author's Wife:	Stories need explanations!
The Author:	You've read a lot of my stories and you know I don't always provide them. Sometimes they're just about weird shit happening.
The Author's Wife:	So you're just going to say that this giant robot just showed up one day and started slaughtering the people of this city at the rate of one a day, and you're not going to explain why.
The Author:	Right. Sometime in the 1880s, I think.
The Author's Wife:	That's stupid!
The Author:	That's one possible interpretation.
The Author's Wife:	What's the possible point of that?
The Author:	Do I have to have one?

· · · ·

My mother and I moved to a duplex in a better neighborhood. I did not understand then that every time the giant robot selected somebody, a sizable deposit was made to the city's treasury and that some of it was earmarked to the victim's immediate survivors, which in our case was my mom and me. In later years my mom said that I also got to go to a better school than I would have otherwise and that I also got a substantial college fund. She didn't think it was an even trade, as she was not that mercenary. But this was just one of those things that happened, if you wanted to live in the city. It was like if you lived in a trailer in the Midwest, you could at any given moment get blown away by a twister; if you lived in a tract house in Los Angeles, you could get wiped out by a mudslide or a grass fire; if you lived in some home on the water, in entire countries, you could spend a random Thursday watching everybody you ever knew being washed away by a tsunami. There was no place to live, anywhere, that was not subject to something. And living here, in this city with enough money from the giant robot's lease payments that it would never have to lay off its firefighters, never have to endure the hell of a sanitation strike, never know an earthquake or a dam break or for that matter the invasion from the evil guys from across the river, was not a bad bargain. One death per day in a city where that was just one of about five hundred from other sources: old age, cancer, slipping on bars of soap, murder, falling down flights of stairs, drug overdoses, choking on Legos, *and* a giant robot in midtown, daily picking a name according to some formula only it understood. Seen statistically, the giant robot was *nothing.*

Still, I was twelve before I could stand to look at the damned thing. My mom had been wise enough to select a house facing the river and not the skyline. When I walked to school, it was with my back to the thing; when I walked back it was with my head down, surveying the cracks in the sidewalk. Sometimes, while playing baseball in the park, I did look up and see the titanic figure in midtown, taller than any of the buildings that surrounded it, and I would have the damnedest sensation that it knew I was looking, that it knew when the sons and daughters of every sacrificed person was looking. I didn't think it felt satisfaction, but neither did I think it was an empty shell, bereft of thought except when the time came for its daily selection; I was certain that whatever it had for a brain was constantly mulling any number of issues, some of which affected who it would pick next. By twelve, I daily shot it the bird.

Between age five and age eighteen I only knew of one person other than my dad who got killed by the robot. This was, I am told, above average. It was not uncommon to know somebody who knew somebody who knew somebody, et cetera, the neighbor's podiatrist's uncle who got nailed by the robot one day, but statistically it was rare to have more than one victim in your inner circle. The second person I knew got taken when I was sixteen. She was a girl two years ahead of me in school. Tisha or Teisa, her name was; I didn't know her except as a gaunt, timid presence in the hallways, who scurried from class to class as if afraid some stalker would slap her on the back of the head with a book. One day in the lunchroom somebody mentioned that Taisha or Teisa had been the robot's designated victim a week or so earlier. Nobody had said anything about it until that day. I had not wondered why she hadn't been showing her face lately. This of course led to the next obvious question, "How did she go?" and here the accounts varied widely, from the guy who said she'd been broiled with a flamethrower to the girl who said she'd been cut into horizontal slices and left stacked in place, like a serving of deli meats. The ewws were respectful, and before it occurred to anybody to point to me and saying, "Hey, Eddie, didn't it zap your Dad too?", everybody started grossing each other out with their own scenarios of really gross ways the robot could kill people, if it ever wanted to, and that went on for a while, until the bell rang and we had to go back to the fucking study of Walt Whitman. That's as close as it ever came to me, after Dad, and I wasn't about to say that I'd been deprived.

The summer after I graduated, I took a bus downtown to revisit the giant robot's neighborhood for the first time since my dad took me. I expected to feel more than I did. I brought a bottle of booze in a paper bag and carried it around with me all afternoon, not knowing when I intended to drink it, and not particularly feeling the need. I passed the out-of-towners taking selfies, the food vendors wheeling the carts in its shadow, the sketch artists offering caricatures for people who wanted their faces superimposed on the robot's blank features, the crazies blaming the robot on the Illuminati or the Jews or the Jewish Illuminati or the Hollywood Liberals or the Jewish Hollywood Liberal Illuminati. I went to the McDonald's tucked against the Robot's ankle and had a Big Mac, thinking of how easy it would be for the thing to twitch just slightly and leave us buried in rubble; not that it ever did that, as it was a polite and considerate genocidal robot, remaining a good neighbor to everybody living adjacent to its personal space. I took out my phone and read about that day's victim: a petty criminal serving a thirty-day stretch in the city jail, who had been eating the second of his day's three allotted bologna sandwiches when the robot's probe snaked it through the widow, inserted a pointy tip into his right eye, and spun like a whisk. It was a pretty nasty way to end a life that had culminated in an arrest for exposing himself on the subway. I felt a twinge, but not much worse than that.

I walked around a bit, went to a movie, came out and found a bench in a little plaza opposite the giant robot's right foot, where I could sit and drink and smoke and contemplate. I received multiple propositions from sex workers of many genders. I was sufficiently intrigued by one of the cuter girls to ask her where we would go, if I said yes. She claimed that there was an alcove in the gap between the robot's big toe and the next toe in line—it had a total of four—where people in her line of work took customers who didn't mind standing up in the dark. It seemed ghoulish to me, so I demurred. She gave me the hotel price, and I said no again.

She told me it was my loss and went away. I took another belt and then another belt after that and as it got darker and colder, I thought about how little it mattered. Then I went over to the robot's heel and pissed on him. A cop saw me and had absolutely no problem with it. The problem was that the robot also had absolutely no problem with it, though I don't know what I expected. The fact of the matter was that when you're pissing on something so large that it doesn't take notice, its failure to take notice is usually a good idea. I felt empty. But there was little to do to feel less empty, so I took the subway home.

∘ ∘ ∘ ∘

The Author's Wife: Another thing. Why don't people just move away?

The Author: I'm sure lots of people do.

The Author's Wife: Who would stay in a city where you can look up and see a giant killer every day?

The Author: People live within full view of volcanoes, don't they?

The Author's Wife: Volcanoes don't kill people every day!

The Author: No, they kill a few hundred at a time, maybe a few thousand. Entire populations live their whole lives within audible range of volcano sirens.

The Author's Wife: Why wouldn't the authorities blow the giant robot up?

The Author: Maybe they've tried.

The Author's Wife: Are you going to say so?

The Author: You mean, am I going to include a scene where the giant robot is assaulted by a fleet of bombers? Where it bellows in rage at all the explosions and uses its gigantic arms to sweep the fleet out of the sky? Where some little kid shrieks, "Gojira! Gojira!" Or maybe, a scene in which some Einstein-haired Professor imparts the knowledge that he has discovered a way in, and tells our square-jawed hero Biff that if he can avoid its internal defenses he can reprogram it to use its giant robot powers for niceness instead of evil?

The Author's Wife: You're making fun of me.

The Author: A little, yeah.

The Author's Wife:	Are you at least going to establish that somebody tried to do something, at some point?
The Author:	It's outside the scope of the story. But, yeah, I suppose that way back in the days when the robot first came down from space or stepped out of the time portal or whatever, and set up shop in the middle of town so it could start killing one person a day, there was mass panic of some sort and people started firing post-Civil War artillery at it, only to realize that nothing they did affected it at all. There's likely a whole novel to be written about that first year or so of the robot's presence in midtown, of the economic shifts that altered the fate of neighborhoods and changed the balance of power in all sorts of ways, like the poorer people and minorities being forced to live closer to it, and so on, until the city finally realized that there was no more disadvantage to living close to it than there is in living close to any other skyscraping structure that blocks out the sun for several hours a day. But, at the time this story begins, it's been in town for about a century and a half, and people have adjusted. It's part of their skyline.
The Author's Wife:	A part of the skyline that kills people.
The Author:	Did you read about that crane that fell off that office building, a year or so ago, and crashed through the top five stories of that condominium across the street? Absolutely horrifying. But if you go to the same town, you will see a bunch of cranes just like it, arrayed on tall buildings, and nobody even looks up.
The Author's Wife:	And that's what your story's about? This huge honking threat that everybody just learns to live with?
The Author:	What do you call the San Andreas Fault?
The Author's Wife:	I would still move away.
The Author:	Again, we live in hurricane country.
The Author's Wife:	It's not the same thing!

The Author:	No, it's not. But, yes, people would move. Many do. Many are the people who had it with big city crime and moved out to the suburbs, or to rural paradises where the sidewalks get rolled up at night. But what kind of story would that be? The protagonist loses his father in a highly traumatic childhood experience and moves on, without consequence, to a small town life with a wife, two point five kids, and a dog? What's the point of that?
The Author's Wife:	What's the point of the story the way you're telling it?
The Author:	That's the kind of thing one discovers while doing it.
The Author's Wife:	Why don't you at least say what the robot thinks it's accomplishing?
The Author:	Well, I don't intend any human being in the story to ever find out, so it's kind of extraneous.
The Author's Wife:	I don't think it's extraneous!
The Author:	Look, if you really insist on a scene from the robot's point of view, I'll give you one. Okay?

• • • •

THE ROBOT'S POINT OF VIEW.

Local time is 14:37. I do not measure time the way the local civilization does but rather according to metrics that would take too long to explain to those more used to that system, not that I plan to make the attempt soon or at any point in the future. Still, I receive all their primitive TV and radio broadcasts and am fully equipped for internet. I routinely cross-reference my internal diaries with their own way of measuring things, not because it matters much to me but because I have nearly infinite computational skill and I might as well. I sometimes section off part of my mind to simulate a typical human being with whom I have conversations. It is a boring activity but, again, I have nothing but time, and so I tell him (or sometimes her) things like, "Well, it's getting about that time again." The human being will protest that I really don't have to kill anybody else today and I will perform the equivalent of a nod and say that this is my function and that with the time being 14:37 (14:38, now), it indeed is getting to be about that time. Sometimes my hypothetical human beings ask me how I decide who I'm going to kill, and how, and I explain that with my nearly instantaneous computation speed I generally don't need to start generating random numbers until the last thousandth of a second before the poor bastard in question ends up being selected. Sometimes they ask me why I have to do it at the same time every day, or if one a day isn't too much, and I explain that given how lightning-fast my thoughts are, that momentary distraction doesn't happen nearly often enough as it is. Honestly, I could eliminate one person every second and the interregnum would still feel like eternity. That I only do this once a day shows tremendous restraint on my part. Every once in a while my simulated human being gets frustrated and shrieks at me, "But why do you do it? What's the point?" And I reply that, since I'm standing around, doing nothing, it would genuinely be too much to ask to expect me to spend all this time here without the consolation of regular activity. It's a hobby, I say. The hypothetical human being, driven beyond all exasperation, will then sometimes yell, "But why are you standing there, at all? Why don't you go somewhere else, where there's something for you to do?" And I say, "That's pretty easy for you to say. I bet you can't even name one." Meanwhile, it's now 14:39.

. . . .

The Author's Wife:	I see what you did there. You made me the voice in the robot's head.
The Author:	Well, you're asking the same questions.
The Author's Wife:	I bet you think I'm annoying, asking you all those questions.
The Author:	Not at all. These questions are useful. I still remember that story I handed you as fait accompli, that you immediately pierced to the core with an intelligent question about character motivation. Because of you I went into the other room and fixed it, and ended up getting nominated for a Nebula. Thank you. That was very helpful.
The Author's Wife:	But you're not fixing what I see as wrong!
The Author:	I'm addressing your issues. I just gave the robot that soliloquy, didn't I?
The Author's Wife:	It answered nothing!
The Author:	It established that the robot is a sentient being of significant intelligence and relatable motivations.
The Author's Wife:	Boredom?
The Author:	Isn't that relatable?

The Author's Wife: You're still pitting your human characters against a massive otherworldly phenomenon that they can neither comprehend nor affect, against which all their struggles are just an exercise in futility.

The Author: And such is life. Right?

· · · ·

I'd been back in town for a couple of years, holding down a couple of jobs and trying to figure out what happened next, wondering if this was all there was, when a friend of mine began badgering me to go to this stinking club to see his stupid band.

Look, if you live in the city, you have an acquaintance with a stupid band. Sometimes it's a good band and sometimes it's a bad one, but it's a stupid band, specifically, when they show up at the day job with fliers and start telling you how awesome it would be if you came out and supported them. It's emotional blackmail, is what it is. It's always seemed to me that if they were any good at all, they wouldn't have to implore people who were just trying to eat their sandwiches to do their duty by supporting the band. Fuck you, what if I don't want to support the band?

I just generally never wanted to head out to a neighborhood I normally wouldn't get caught dead in just so I could pay the cover and buy the two drink minimum and probably not get out without buying the CDs or t-shirts at the door, and I didn't want to do any of those goddamned things.

So it was with this one guy, called himself Oz—which he carefully explained was not short for Oswald, but an actual reference to the fictional country, and that also required him to explain that he was not talking about the Judy Garland movie, which was corporate bullshit, but the L. Frank Baum novels, and honestly I saw him go through this rigamarole every time a new hire wandered into the break room, an awful lot of punishment for anybody to go through when it was simpler to just leave it with him saying "Call me Oz," and you replying, "Okay, if that's what you want, I'll call you Oz." Oz had a band that I really needed to get out there and support, and I kept blowing him off, which was only reasonable because after all that explanation of his name I'd sure as shit had more than enough of his lyrics. Anyway, I'd managed to say no the first two times they played and I was on a scheduled vacation for their third but then the fourth rolled on and the guy showed up at my corner of the office saying, "Come on, it'll be fantastic," and I realized with sinking heart that I couldn't put it off any longer without being a dick.

It probably would have been more honest to just bite the bullet and be a dick, because at the damn least it meant that I would never be asked again, but I needed the job and didn't want to be the object of stink-eye every day, so I said, what the hell, I'll see you there.

It was a basement club, a full flight below the street, no elevator and likely little in the way of fire exits, possibly illegal if the city ever got around to inspecting the joint, which was iffy even in a city that had never needed to cut municipal services. Even when the economy is good, there are still things like bribes, backlog, and bureaucracies that don't give a shit. The building was set back from the street and protected by those concrete crash barriers public places erect to prevent truck bombings, which led to silly thoughts about just what kind of eccentric terrorists would pick that crappy club as their target of choice. When I got downstairs, the place was dark in the manner of rooms that by design don't ever light up enough to make a difference. It was long and narrow with a stage at the far end, and though the city had a smoking ban, the ceiling was swathed in a thick haze that seemed more dust than the product of tobacco, clove, or pot. It smelled off. I picked a stool as far from the stage as possible, to facilitate an escape if necessary.

How the hell was I to know their band, GRO, was an acronym for Giant Robot Orchestra?

They came out wrapped in a substance that looked like aluminum foil, their faces painted a metallic silver, pre-recorded audio blasting various mechanical and hydraulic noises as they jerked about like automatons. They had a fan base, surprisingly, because at the moment they finished their walk-out song and froze in place, arms akimbo, the place went wild with woos. I could only sit on my stool at the bar, the one I had chosen for proximity to the door in case I wanted to get out as quickly as it now seemed I wanted to, and listen for the duration of the three songs that struck me as a reasonable definition of giving them a fair chance. Their second song was all about the robot leaving its habitual place and doing a choreographed dance-stomp over all the ant-like pedestrians in the street, "Stomp Stomp I Do The Stomp," and the second had something to do with the robot acquiring corporate sponsors. The third was about a girl who nightly used one of the robot's flailing murder-tentacles as a sex toy, and in the last verse actually included a couplet about her seeing red when it crushed your head, and at that moment I got off the stool and marched out the front door and up the stairs to the street.

I got as far as the sidewalk, where a bunch of refugees had gathered, looking up at the place in the skyline where the giant robot eclipsed everything else. They were smoking and bullshitting and listening to the percussion, just the percussion, as that was the only part of the music that carried past the stairs. As percussion, it wasn't half bad. It was colder than I'd expected, as the temperature had dropped within the last half hour or so. I lit a cigarette and stood there fuming in that manner and in my own, when a petite Asian girl (Korean, though I did not know that yet), with stubbly white hair and a studded black leather jacket came out, hopped up on one of the concrete barriers and lit her own smoke, leaving it between her lips to smolder without much in the way of obvious inhalation. Her eyes were fixed on the outline of the giant robot.

And suddenly, I *knew*. "Who was it?"

She glanced at me, and suddenly, *she* knew. "You first."

"My dad."

"My older sister."

"I was five."

"I wasn't even born yet. I was conceived as replacement kid."

"That sucks."

She shrugged. "It's not a contest. I'm sorry about your dad."

"I'm sorry about your sister."

Silence intervened. This was, I'd learned, a natural consequence of having a loved one who got killed by a giant robot. The fact of it, when mentioned, tended to be the speed-bump in the center of conversations, the one that cut off all potential topics up to that point and prevented the planting of any conversational seeds up after that point. I wanted to say more, but anything else might have felt too much like a pick-up strategy, even now that the thought didn't seem like a terrible one. After a moment, I said, "They don't suck. I wouldn't mind listening to them if they played anything else."

"No," she agreed. "They don't suck, and I'm only here because the guy on drums kept handing out fliers at work until I finally surrendered."

"I'm not going to buy the CD."

"And I'm not going to buy the t-shirt."

"Fuck them."

"Royally."

We smoked a bit, and after a while, she said, "Wanna get the hell out of here and talk about literally anything else?"

This was, it turned out, how we met.

We were together when we found out that another giant robot had appeared, standing on the water in Hong Kong harbor.

• • • •

The Author's Wife:	For a few seconds there I thought this whole story was going to be a massive exercise in a Meet-Cute.
The Author:	It was beginning to feel that way to me, too.
The Author's Wife:	It would have been unworthy of you.
The Author:	I've always hated the kind of story where there's some massive threat to life and limb and we see a lot of people die and it all turns out to be okay in the end because the two people we care about most embrace as newly-minted lovers in the rubble.
The Author's Wife:	Well, these cute kids getting together would have certainly been an adequate payoff for five thousand six hundred words of a giant robot standing in the middle of town, executing people!
The Author:	Sarcasm, right?
The Author's Wife:	I still don't know where you're going with this.
The Author:	Look, the problem with this premise is that most of the places where it can go, or where stories like it have gone, are places where I don't want this one to go. I don't want an ending where the robot speaks a sentence out loud that suddenly explains everything. I don't want the guy and girl to get married and settle down in domestic bliss, where that is handed out as a reward for enduring everything that came before. I don't want an action-packed skyscraper-toppling climax where the robot built by the humans marches down from upstate and takes on whatsitsname in a battle of titans. All of these would be betrayals of the central conceit, that the robot is just a thing that happens to be, that the poor schmucks at street level need to get used to sublimating as a daily threat. Like terrorism, for instance.
The Author's Wife:	Life needs to go on.
The Author:	That's right.
The Author's Wife:	So your protagonist and Blonde Asian Chick don't stay together.

The Author: I'm not actually going to chart the rise and fall of their relationship, no. I think it gets pretty hot and heavy for a bit, that they maybe spend a little time living together, but that after a while they both realize that this commonality between them, this shared past with the giant robot, doesn't amount to enough to qualify them as life partners. Ultimately, they will meet other people, move on, maybe stay in touch as friends for as long as it takes for staying in touch to become more trouble than it's worth. That's messy and that prevents the grotesquery of reducing the giant robot to matchmaker.

The Author's Wife: Except that now you've set up a second robot, and through it implied that this is a full-scale, if slow-motion, invasion.

The Author: Yeah, and you know, I don't want this to be the direction I go from here, either. I don't want this to devolve to a long list of cities where fresh giant robots have shown up. Even if there are more coming, it took so many years for the second that the appearance of the third is likely outside the scope of the plot. It's more dread than I want to deal with, and not what the story feels like it's about. So let's just say, boom: This second giant robot is the only other giant robot there is, and it doesn't disrupt the daily routine of Hong Kong any more violently than this one disrupts the city of this story.

The Author's Wife: I still don't see the point of all this.

The Author: I have one, honestly.

· · · ·

My mom had died a few months back, talking about Dad to her very last breath, and between that and the crash-and-burn of my only night out with a member of the opposite sex since breaking up with Eun-Ae, I'd been at odds and ends for a few weeks. I guess I was depressed. I don't know if it was clinical depression, but it sure as hell was the sense that my life had fallen into a permanent rut. It was cold out and if I hate anything beyond the giant robot, it's the cold, but I was in danger of spending the weekend barricaded inside my three hundred square feet . . . again.

So I bundled up and went down the street and had a hot dog on that place on the corner with the really good relish and walked the five blocks to the big park, where there was always something going on. What I found was a crappy little band that I listened to for a little while, not because they were great but because they were enthused; sometimes that's enough, when you're not in the mood for smiling, yourself. They were worth applauding just for their willingness to play in the cold, especially from the point of view of a guy who'd been flirting with agoraphobia. They were life, asserting itself as a thing that didn't necessarily suck, that was worth going out to find when four walls and Amazon Prime seemed preferable.

Then I walked a little farther and found an art installation that somebody had set up. It was called *Be The Giant Robot* and it was a simplified 3-D model of midtown, mostly the major buildings, that came complete with two foot-shaped outlines in the places that corresponded to the robot's feet. You were invited to stand in those places and see what it was like to be the robot, master of all it surveyed. I might not have done it if there'd been a long line but someone told me that it had been around for a couple of months already and would soon be removed, so the combination of a short wait and the urgency that went along with the awareness that the opportunity would be gone soon gave me the added push I needed. I put my shoes on those scuffed places and looked around at the major buildings and I thought about how goddamned insignificant it all probably looked to that naked chrome asshole. *And yet, he's alone*, I thought, trying to see it his way. And it didn't make me feel one bit better because I was alone, too: alone at work, alone in my social life, alone without a family: hell, alone even with myself, because I was no company worth keeping.

I glanced at midtown, the real midtown, where the real bastard was still visible in the distance, arms on his hips like Superman. It's funny. You can always see him if you're looking that way, but after a while your eyes develop a kind of blindness to him. You forget he's there. You forget what he does at 3:00 p.m. every day. He becomes just a thing. And of course you can always get the daily casualty, but unless it's some especially tragic one like some elementary school kid waiting for the bus home or some bride in the middle of her wedding reception, or something personal like my dad, it's just background noise, really. Something you never pay attention to, compared to how much attention you need to pay to, you know, getting where you needed to be, doing whatever you needed to be.

I left the art installation and walked the path around the lake, happy when the route put my back to the figure on the horizon, but if I told you that I had stopped thinking about him I'd be lying. Mostly, he was at the center of all my self-pity. My dad was part of it, as he always was. I'd never been able to lose the expression on his face, that little over-enthused joy he took in sharing that board game with me, replaced instantly with the pulp the son of a bitch had made of him. That had never left me; I suppose I've never been able to trust fun, of any sort, let alone happiness, of any sort, since. But I wasn't just thinking about him. I was thinking about the things you think about, when you're pushing thirty and your life is going nowhere. There's an old song someone once played for me, with the refrain, "Is that all there is?" And that question had been making more and more sense to me, lately: that it was, that if there was anything else there was nothing I could grab on to, not even now when I could begin to feel the time drifting away in big chunks.

Suicide did not enter into it, not in any deep way. It wasn't that black a mood. I think that unless my life ever took a turn darker than anything that's ever happened before, I wouldn't ever entertain that as a possibility. I didn't want to kill myself. I wanted what I felt to be over. If that meant willing a sniper's bullet into being, or hoping that some big truck blew a tire and hopped the sidewalk, so be it. I started daydreaming about the ways it could happen, the relief it would be. And so, by the time I could see the giant robot again, I was prepared for the thought that it would even be okay if it was him; if at 3:00 p.m. today he sent that tentacle of his wailing across the miles to pierce me where I stood, I would meet my end relieved. It would be right, and it would be just.

There was a permanent snack stand, selling salted pretzels and other junk food, just off the path near where I would have completed a perfect circle. I was not hungry for anything but I wanted to sit at one of the steel tables and so I bought one of the pretzels and sat, alone, watching the giant robot in the distance. He was so big he dominated the whole damn city, and through it the whole damn world. It was 2:49 p.m. and I found myself uncannily certain that today was my day: that even if I turned my back and ran to the nearest curb and got a taxi and ordered the driver to whisk me out of range, that range would only be extended, in order to accommodate my distance. I would go in order to fulfill the bastard's great cosmic plan, the way my father had, and it would be the exclamation point at a life that had reached a dead end anyway.

I ate my pretzel, one eye on my phone as the minutes ticked down to the hour that punctuated the city's history, every damn day. Ten minutes away. Then nine. Then five, and I closed my eyes and tried to count down what remained, without any wired help, surprised by how hard my heart was pounding. *This is stupid*, I thought, and it was, even though I remained no less certain that I was the next. It occurred to me that this was my last pretzel, as the hot dog had been my last hot dog, as Eun-Ae had been the last person who had ever given me the impression that she could be with me for the rest of my life, and none of this seemed fitting at all; it just seemed goddamned unfair, and the knowledge that there was nothing I could do to change that outcome made me not relieved, but angry.

After a long time in self-imposed darkness, I opened my eyes and checked the time again.

It was 3:03.

The death app had not updated yet. But by about seven minutes later it had. It was somebody I'd never heard of, a pedestrian a mere four blocks from the robot's left foot. He was a tragedy, no doubt. But the robot hadn't gotten me today and wasn't going to, any more than it would probably get me tomorrow, or the day after. Maybe someday it would. But if it did, I wouldn't receive any advance warning from clairvoyance. Or ever be able to exert influence, positive or negative, with the power of my own self-pity.

For no reason at all, this made me feel incrementally lighter. I didn't know what the hell I was going to do about it, but I could enjoy the feeling for a bit.

Until then I bought some hot chocolate, to warm the way home.

AND NOW, A PREVIEW OF COMING ATTRACTIONS

I have experienced some tastes of my afterlife as a crustacean.

In it, I am one of many, on a beach with purple sand abutting a sea that could be water but might be some other liquid entirely, beneath stars that seem larger and brighter than any I see in the night sky now. The effect is very alien, but I have no idea whether the place really looks that strange, because I am looking at it with the eyes of a creature not human, which may be seeing it in spectra my human self cannot measure. Maybe whatever I am then adds all those colors; maybe what I perceive is an error in translation between the human being I am now and the crustacean I will be then.

Either of these two explanations can also apply to the constant high-pitched hum that never goes away there, which strikes me as the kind of thing that should be maddening but which to my crustacean self is a beloved and necessary part of the environment, a part of the ambience I treasure and need in order to live. It is the constant background music of my life in a shell, and maybe I describe it wrongly. I am a man, and as a crustacean my mind works differently than the mind of a man. It is slower, and harsher, and yet in some ways more elevated and perceptive. It is wise in a way I cannot be, while naïve in others I'm not.

As a crustacean I am low to the ground, and spiny, and I survive by using my powerful claws to crack open the shells that the high tide deposits on my beach, and that always contain soft succulent things I extract with a long, flute-like extremity that is most like, but not quite, a tongue. The stored heat in the sand keeps my body temperature regulated and also sets my stomach acids to breaking down whatever I consume. Dragging myself across that sand is a sensual pleasure that I deeply miss whenever that alien world goes away and I am stuck in the body of a human being again.

When I return to being me, I cannot quite summon the thrill of crustacean life, just as I know that it upon remembering me cannot quite summon the thrill of being a soft layer of upright meat, over internal skeleton, wearing a tie and walking around in shoes. This is at some point in my future, after I am born to that life, after I am raised in it, after I live that way for a while; after I have spent some time processing alien thoughts with alien wiring, after I can no longer summon the memories of being me in any real detail. I do, however, like to imagine that it is able to sense itself being watched by me its past self, and that it sends a message back, through all that distance, that in people-speak reads as, "Do not worry. It will be all right."

- - - -

I get these previews more often nowadays, because I am dying.

It is an astonishing thought. We all know we will die someday, in no large part because we receive this preview of our future as crustacean or flying thing or swimming thing or rooted thing, but also because we see the disappearances of those we know, the aged relatives and unlucky friends and the celebrated people who strut in notoriety for a decade or so and then perish from misadventure or actuarial chance. The President of the United States disappeared a few years ago, felled by an assassin's bullet, gone so fast that her body never struck the ground. I should know that if it happened to her, a terrestrial ending of some kind will come to me, but until my doctor told me that my time here was short, I held on to that irrational belief we all have that I was somehow an exception, that I would be here, on this planet, a human being, forever. Then I got the first taste of my future life as crustacean that I've gotten since childhood; the first of many, as it turns out. I am there often now, more often today since yesterday and no doubt more often still, by tomorrow. "Flickering," we call it. I am dying, and so I flicker, like some ghostly comedian in an old-time silent movie; a few more minutes every day.

The cause will be an aneurism. It is deep in the brain where no surgeon can get to it, and it is getting larger, and from time to time I suffer little deaths, a second or two in duration, at least once as long as
a minute, and each time, witnesses say, I do what people do on dying
and vanish from this world, only to pass back into existence confused
and disoriented and still thinking like a crustacean. I had some health
problems as a child and experienced it then, but not for a long time until
an isolated incident at work about sixteen months ago; a few minutes
of crustacean followed by the sight of all my co-workers bent over me,
looking concerned and, I think, among those who have grown tired of
life, envious. Now it happens at least once a day, sometimes many times,
and I can no longer work or drive. I fade out and then I fade back in, on
the couch, or in our bed, and Analise shows the relief that this time, at
least, I have returned. Sometimes tears fall, because she knows that I go
where she cannot follow. It's been established. After she dies, she'll be a
golden ape.

• • • •

On the day I found out that death was coming, I surrendered my driver's
license, because the flash-forwards would be happening more and more
often now and it would not do to disappear from existence when I was
in my car, barreling down an expressway at seventy. You hear of that happening all the time; one car wanders into the wrong lane and takes out
another, and when the authorities get around to pulling out survivors
there is no one behind the steering wheel of the car that lost control.

So I gave up my driver's license as the law required, leaving my car
in a parking lot for someone to retrieve later and because I was not yet
ready to face Analise with the news, called up the father I hadn't seen
for four years or spoken to at all in two. He was still living out on the
island, cashing his retirement checks and posting angry screeds on the
political blogs. To my surprise he agreed to see me, and I took an Uber
out to the island, passing a familiar neighborhood of attached houses and
another of tenements to another where little clapboard homes with front
porches sat side by side with lot lines so narrow that the spaces between
them were, though planted with resentful strips of grass, less lawns than
alleys. That was where we'd lived and where he still hung on. As the Uber
dropped me off, I saw that he had come out on the porch to wait for me,
his oxygen tank at his left and the table bearing his ashtray and empty
beer cans on his right. He nodded at me, but didn't wave, and I didn't
blame him, because a wave might have testified to a closeness we'd never

known. I got out and made my way along the cracked walk to the three stairs leading up to the porch and said, "Hello, Dad," and he nodded and got straight to the point of the matter, "Hey, Alan, who died?" I told him it was nobody yet and my voice cracked just enough that he figured it out and said, "Aw, hell. Want a beer?"

Alcohol was one of the things I'd been warned against, but there are traditions that must be respected, and so I said yes. He handed me a can and I peeled the top and took a sip and tried not to wince. Even if I was a beer guy, and I never have been, my father is the kind of beer guy who buys the cheapest, most generic brand, disdaining all issues of taste in favor of the ability to create a daily wall of dead soldiers without breaking the bank or muddying the issue with questions like flavor. He patted the folding chair beside him, inviting me to sit and watch the birds. I had no interest in birds and so I repositioned the chair so that it faced him and then sat.

We studied each other for a little bit: him with his fresh jowls and yellow-parchment complexion, myself with sunken cheeks and the complexion of a whiter shade of paper. He smiled and showed flattened teeth and said, "Cancer?"

"No, Dad."

"Shame," he said. "You could have had the crab and then been one. Not that I wish cancer on you; I'm just saying. What is it?"

I told him and for a bit I endured his questions about the nature of my ailment and its ensuing prognosis, something he didn't quite get, but was willing to take an interest in. He ran out of questions at about the time my bladder ran out of space. He told me that the door was open and I went in, hitting what amounted to a solid wall of haze and rotten food stink. He had gotten worse about airing out the house since the last time I saw him. But I persevered, made my way to the downstairs bathroom and, gagging again because he hadn't flushed this morning, found relief. On my way out, I got the bagged food garbage from the can in the kitchen and brought it out to the can at the curb before returning to him. He didn't thank me for taking out the trash, just asked if I wanted another beer. But the wariness had entered his eyes, really, that and the alcoholic math pitting the obligations of hospitality against the finite nature of supply. I said I was okay, handed him a couple of hundreds and used the app on my phone to order another car. At which point he said something he'd been saying since my childhood close call with a speeding car gave me the first glimpse of my afterlife, something he'd found quite funny when I was a kid and that had developed a certain pathetic flavor, since.

"I'm gonna be a maggot."

* * * *

Death is, I tell myself, nothing to be afraid of. This is why the good Lord makes sure we all get these previews, at moments when death seems imminent; why my mother first learned she was going to be some kind of carnivorous alien sunflower at age seventeen, or why my brother Dan spent half his time in the war, blinking in and out of existence to experience flashes of his future incarnation as sentient virus.

The theological argument has always been that God provides these previews to prove his love, to assure us that our souls are eternal and that we only change state, like water turning to ice or vapor. It isn't much of a comfort to a guy like Dan who understood that he would live out his next life causing peritonitis in some alien bovine's large intestine. By the time he pulled the pin on himself, he was saying that it could only be an improvement on this goddamned planet. He was a drinker like Dad by then, vacillating between random bursts of drunken hilarity and random bursts of inebriated misery with little in the way of transition, sometimes swinging from one extreme to the other multiple times a minute, the absurdity of his destination manifesting with his own favorite joke, that he was going to move to a condo up a cow's ass. When he finally disappeared, nobody was watching, but the sheer amount of booze around the place suggested that he'd drunk himself right into his new and even more septic existence. But at least we know where that was, and it's been so long since then that maybe he's died again, once or more than once, and now lives as a species he could be proud of.

Mom, wasted in bed without the capacity to sit up, used to choke that she wanted to be that sunflower already, wanted to feel the rich nutrients in the soil rising up through her stalk, to fuel another day's growth while the golden light from above made every inch of her tingle like fire; and over the last few weeks she spent more and more of her time living that life, sometimes gone for so long that even the doctors gazing down at her empty bed wondered if she had already passed through the veil. Then she would reappear and say, "Oh, not here again," with something like despair, and though I knew that it was the pain talking, she would also always be upset at herself for expressing such resentment in front of me, her dutiful son, both happy and appalled that her existence as human being still had some hold on her, even when all it could offer was torment. But her alien sunflower life gave us much to talk about. As a human, she didn't have the vocabulary to fully explain what an alien sunflower thinks, what being one feels like and what politics rule its traffic with others of its kind, but she tried, and there were times when she seemed about to come up with a perfect metaphor before she turned transparent, the wrinkles on her pillow clearly visible through her pale features, and I knew that the sunflower life was pulling at her again, more real to her at that moment than I was.

. . . .

Nobody ever remembers their past lives, though some claim to; that's just nonsense. We may get little dream-images, impressions of flying or of burrowing underground or otherwise behaving in ways alien to our lives now. They may be memories. But who knows? There is no way to tell for sure.

But I tell Analise that wherever I was when that version of myself who was an alien mouse or hippogriff or slime mold in the life before this one first tasted the proximity of death and caught a glimpse of its future existence as myself, it must have been excited to see that its future included a creature as gorgeous as herself.

She smiles. She's good at smiling; she lights up the room when she does. She has a laugh like music, and when we make love, she frequently bursts into laughter, as if what we do together is the funniest thing that ever happened on this Earth. When I ask why she says, "Because it *is* funny. Don't you know that?" She says that the golden apes, whose ways she knows well, laugh uproariously through the act, and that her own human hilarity during the act can mean that they have extended their influence into the life she lives now, or it might be a peculiarity of her nature that may have influenced where she will end up after this life.

Analise teaches natural science and in particular she teaches exobiology, a profoundly speculative body of knowledge that has only congealed into a science because of the fragmentary reports we compile from the reported lives to come. Some witnesses, she tells her fifth-graders, must surely be lying. People who say that one day they'll be some noble jungle cat, lord of all the lesser creatures around them, might be concocting that to avoid admitting that instead they'll be some form of sentient alien moss, giving off clouds of toxic vapor while adhering to a wall in a cave. If people lie on their résumés, they'll lie about the lives to come. Rare indeed are the grim, honest reports like my father's, the future as alien larva subsisting on carrion. Surely, some people must glamorize.

But some forms show up more than once, and therefore have the ring of confirmation: the swimmers and the fliers and the predators and the wispy philosophers and the things that we cannot quite understand because the people whose reports we got could only describe them in the most fragmentary ways. It is from her that I know that my crustacean future seems to be unprecedented, and therefore still subject to many uncertainties. I may be the first human being whose trajectory intersects that particular world. Who knows?

Either way, future golden apes, like Analise, are fairly common. Maybe one percent of the human population. It is like a common blood type, really. And among those who don't know, it's a desired destination. Who wouldn't want to be a glorious golden ape?

Analise knows that she will be a golden ape because of childhood sleep apnea that put her at strong risk for sudden death; an ailment that my in-laws say once made her flicker in her crib like an old-time movie or like a light in danger of going out, which of course she was. The first time she completely went away for more than a second or so, leaving only the indentation in the comforter to prove that she'd ever been there, my mother-in-law went a little crazy with fear that her darling baby would never come back and would instead stay in whatever alien land she'd gone to, living her new life as alien analogue to worm or mushroom or eagle forever with only this slightest brief taste of life as human child to sometimes disturb her dreams. Then Analise came back, coughing but gurgling in evident delight, testifying that her destination had been perceived by her infant self as a good place, and giving cause for hope throughout every subsequent attack until, in time, she obtained language and was able to explain that she had another life as a "blonde monkey."

In time, she confirmed that she meant "golden ape," the apnea went away, and she experienced no further tastes of that future until one day in her twenties when she choked on a fragment of chicken bone and disappeared in the middle of a crowded restaurant, and then found herself in the upper branches of a mile-high tree beneath looming scarlet clouds. That lasted all of three minutes before she popped back into terrestrial existence, gasping heavily. She knew a golden ape lover in that three minutes, and she still speaks of the experience with dreamy eyes, because no one who has ever had a taste of that future can ever describe it in terms that don't make it sound like paradise.

* * * *

Early in our dating life, she said, "I had long furry arms like an orangutan's, but it was really nothing like that. I wasn't built like an orangutan, for one thing. I had six limbs, not four, and they all came together in a torso that didn't have much to it; not so much a trunk as an intersection. I think I may have been more like a spider. But there were others around me, talking, and I knew what they were saying, and it was beautiful. We were philosophers. We lived so high up that tree that the forest floor was a rumor, and still so far below the canopy that sunlight struck us only as little needles of light as slight as pinky fingers, and there were these constant mists that swirled around us, perfumed by all the flowers, and what I remember most about it was that it made me horny; it's making me horny now, just describing it, but it's not me the human woman feeling that way, it's me remembering myself as that ape, and being more at home there than I ever was as a person. Do you feel that way, as your crab?"

She had a bad habit of calling my crustacean self a crab, when in fact I had told her that it was really its own thing and as hard to categorize as a crab as her next life was categorized as an ape. We all do that, with our merely human tongues. After our flash-forwards, we say that we became a sunflower like my mom and say that it was not really a sunflower. We say that we became a dolphin or a fish or a horse and then we hasten to add, "only not really like that," because of course it's not like that; what we're headed for is something that never evolved on Earth, that cannot be categorized in the terms of terrestrial evolution. But the comparisons we apologize for still exist. So she says "golden ape," laughing that even there, she's still blonde; and I say "crustacean," and add that I always did like the beach. And these days, like Mom, I spend increasing time in that future place, aware with every even brief visit that I am fast approaching the moment when I go there and do not come back; when I vanish in place and do not reappear, any more than Mom or Dan reappeared.

"Yes," I said simply. "I feel that way, as a crab."

Though I do not think the crustacean I will become thinks of sex, much. There is certainly a reproductive impulse, but I don't think the sex/pleasure connection works on that species the way it does for human beings, or for golden apes. The pleasure I derive from my tastes of life as that species is more connected to the specific sensual impulse of warm sand, heating up my insides and making the food in my stomach break down the way it must. As a crustacean, it is the sand that turns me on; the sand that gives me the crustacean equivalent of orgasm. But I did not say so, when we discussed this, because I was focused on the prospect of getting her into bed for the first time and thought it better to accentuate the drives we shared in this incarnation than those that would be present in the next. And so we had kinky spider-ape snapping crustacean sex, laughing about it, her saying ook-ook when it seemed appropriate and me saying some witless thing about getting my claws on her, but there were just two human beings there, really; two who got to know that which was also present, even though it wouldn't always be. And then we did it again, and again a couple of nights after that, and again on multiple occasions after that, and for a time neither of us had any close calls immediate enough to manifest our futures again; and for a time, we were just people; a process I now, without volition, abandon multiple times a day. I am a man becoming less and less a human being and more and more a scuttler on sand.

. . . .

One day when she is out shopping and I am stuck at home watching a classic movies channel, the world goes away with a hard snap and, I, during the black transition, think that this is it. It is so sudden it could only be true death, and so she must be coming home to an empty house, my presence marked only by the indentation I leave on the couch. I find myself on that alien beach, surrounded by the others of my kind, and it is so vivid that it puts all my memories as human being in the shadow, and I also find out that life as this crustacean thing is more complicated than all my past previews suggested, because my kind is at war. The alien software driving whatever my new crustacean species uses to house its mind is not talented at counting, but there must be thousands of us crowding those sands, and we are marching, or as close to marching as we are built for, and we are advancing on creatures not quite like us, who I have the innate knowledge of as ancient enemies who are a direct threat to our existence, and who must be repelled in this, their perennial effort to claim our perfect feeding ground for themselves. They are, I think, white lobster-things, though again the differences between the human taxonomic vocabulary and the vocabulary of this creature I am make the precise classification impossible. They are without number. They are perceived by me as terrifyingly evil, but I know that they have been defeated before, and that they can be defeated again, as bad as it looks now. They must be. When we close with them, our claws clatter against theirs, and both sides snip and tear, and the beach turns the color of blood—a specific shade I have no human analogue for—as carapaces are punctured and internal meat is ripped out and as twitching limbs continue to thrash like things that still have input into their own fates. The scent of carnage is overpowering, and as we all fight for our lives, the stench draws the birds, which are, much like we're not really crustaceans but something that reminds human beings of crustaceans, not birds but things that are easiest to explain as an analogue to sea gulls. They swoop down in great numbers, the sky turning to night, and they land on anything at all disabled and tear at us with their beaks, claiming whatever food they can. I see a companion impaled through the midsection, screeching in the precise way we do when death comes for us, and for one heartbeat of profound disconnection I think of all this in the way that a human being might, wondering if any of these damned birds were ever once people, and if any one of them is experiencing this moment from the point of view of some piece of shit having a near-death experience on Earth, and thinking of this assault upon our innocent kind as something to look forward to, something that will render his or her current life as librarian or taxi driver or brain surgeon a pale afterthought, once it has reached this moment. Ignoring the white-lobster enemy I launch myself at the gull-thing instead, and as it pecks at me, I wrap my powerful claws around its feathered throat.

Then there is that moment of disconnect again and I find myself looking up at Analise, who is weeping, who is saying that she thought I was gone for sure this time, and no woman on Earth has ever looked more beautiful, and no woman ever married to a man who loved her has ever looked more alien. I cannot make sense of her features. What are those glossy, wet objects set in hollows, beneath that hanging brow? What is that pale protruding triangle? That gaping abyss beneath, lined in glossy red coloring, what is that, and what is that worm I thought I saw inhabiting it? She is alien terror on a Lovecraftian scale, and then in a flash, it is just my wife, resolving in the way any incomprehensible sight does once it returns to making sense. She lowers her forehead to mine, and for a time we weep together, happy that this part of our respective eternal stories is not over.

But I am also thinking that I have been robbed of my revenge on that gull.

* * * *

Dr. Patel sees me every few weeks to check on the progress of my deterioration. He says that I am doing as well as he had any right to expect. That is the way he frames it, as a prospect measured by his own degree of hope, and I do not know whether to feel my condition honored or the object of condescension. I have gotten over-sensitive, I suppose, in these the past few months of my life, and it takes an active act of charity to resolve it with the rationalization that it shows how much he cares.

He also says that these regular measurements are academic, because aside from some palliative care, there is little he can do. The end is coming. Every day I live damages me; every moment I vanish and spend another few minutes as crustacean brings me closer to my permanent transition. I have, as a dying man, already undergone a permanent metamorphosis, in a way. I have already stopped being the guy who showers and gets dressed and eats breakfast and only then wakes up the wife whose shift starts an hour after mine. I have stopped being the guy who goes to work and sees himself as a useful person. I am now the man who drifts off early in the evening, sleeps an additional three hours and still wakes up tired, who has little energy to spend on the activities that take up the rest of the day. The metamorphosis will continue and I will someday soon stop being the guy who walks upright and breathes oxygen. I will instead become something else, something I have made no secret about longing to become; and that might happen later today or it might happen six months from now, and my discussions with Patel have become more about amelioration, about palliative treatments, about therapies to help me put aside what I am and come to terms with what I will be.

Still, he does what he always does to measure my ailment's progress. He shines a light in my eyes, noting the dilation intervals of both pupils. He tests my reflexes. He asks me if there's any pain, not that he expects any pain; the brain doesn't feel it, he says. He asks if I'm keeping my spirits up. I say I am, and he says that's good.

He does this and as the examination continues, I watch him more and more closely, and increasingly confirm something that I first perceived on the day when he told me I was terminal; that it is all rote, all professionalism unpolluted by passion, all the behavior of a man who, though good at his job, feels absolutely none of it. I am more and more certain that he actually envies me, that his emotional investment is actually more in the life to come than in the life he's currently stranded in.

I ask him if he has learned the form of his own next incarnation.

Something strange comes into his eyes, and he says, "An elephant."

Only, he now corrects himself, not an elephant. The creature he will be reborn as has two trunks, a plate of bone protecting the back of the neck, and a pair of additional eyes at the base of the spine, forever searching for predators who might be approaching from behind. And the plants, he says, the plants. They look nothing like anything to be found on the African savannah. But oh, the way they taste . . . and then he seems to remember where he is, and who he's speaking to, and that professional façade slides back into position, and we are once again doctor and patient, with nothing but the facts of the case between us.

Then I say, "Has anybody ever succeeded in changing it?"

He frowns. "What do you mean, changing it?"

"The destination species."

"I thought you were looking forward to being a crustacean."

"I am. From the tastes I've gotten, it's quite enjoyable."

"And?"

"I've had another glimpse and learned more. They have wars. Very bloody wars. I was on one of their battlefields and it was . . . well, total, absolute carnage. Savagery, really. What if that's not what I want in a life? What if I want to be a golden ape and live with Analise? Is there any way I can change my destination? Has anybody ever done that?"

I recognize the look on his learned face. It's the physician's default compassionate look, the same one he wore when he pronounced my condition inoperable. He places his hand on my shoulder and he tells me that people have tried; that they've gone to hypnotists and they've practiced intense meditation and they've spent all their time picturing the destination they want over the destination they've learned, and in some cases it has eaten up all their energies in what time they had left.

I ask if it's ever worked, even once, and the default compassionate look intensifies and he says that when he was a child there was a common belief that if you die in a dream you die in real life, and it was bandied about as a fact, until somebody finally asked the logical question: Even if that was true, how would we even know, when nobody's ever returned from permanent death to report it?

I say I don't know, and he says,

"Well, then, the same is true about changing your destination. There are posited treatments, offered by therapists and drug companies and religious leaders, and they all claim to work, but they all have the same thing in common: Nobody's ever come back from their new life as an alien lemur to say they got to be that instead of an alien pilot fish. Nobody's ever said that they've arranged to be human for the second time in a row, told us that they when they come back they'll give us the secret password to confirm it, then twenty years later, having been reborn and progressed to adulthood, walked back into the laboratory to say, it's me, Phil, and as I told you before, the crow flies at midnight. It's never happened. Not even once. My personal belief is that it cannot. We are stuck being what we are and we are stuck being whatever we'll soon become, until that cycle ends and we start another random existence, somewhere else. It's just the way things are. Stop worrying about it."

I can't help asking, "But what if it's terrible?"

* * * *

Once trapped at home again, I start reading up and find among the reams of inevitable know-nothing bullshit an interesting philosophical experiment, by a thinker who I've never encountered before. Imagine, she said, that all the afterlives we've documented over the centuries were reduced to an irreducible binary, one good and one bad. Posit that everyone who lives ultimately goes to one or the other, based on some factor that could be measured and even influenced: with virtue, for instance. Imagine further that the price we paid for this simplicity, this promise that the best of us will get to enjoy joyous reunions with their loved ones, was the absence of certainty; that we honestly had no way of knowing whether this was a true promise or just something that somebody made up.

This would be terrible, she said. Our whole lives as human beings would be spent bargaining. What would be the point of that? If I'm going to be some scaled flying squirrel and if I know that from the very first time I experience uncertainty about my immediate survival, don't I then lose what would otherwise be an overwhelming fear of death? Am I not blessed by knowing?

And what if it's not good? I ask, silently. *What if your flying squirrels use their gliding capacity to invade the branches of other squirrels, and slaughter them in the places where they nest? What if this is a daily part of the life you are destined to be born to and there's nothing to be done about it? Wouldn't the uncertainty be preferable?*

The tract offers no answer. Nor does the one I read next, or the one after that. I fall into a depression, and for the first time since my ailment was diagnosed, I go four full days without a flash-forward. It is like I erased my future as crustacean and replaced it with nothing at all, or something so terrible that I cannot be allowed the advance preview, as it would destroy me. And I know that the philosopher is right. The uncertainty is worse.

* * * *

My father dies.

We assume he dies. You can't know for sure that somebody's died unless you see them vanish and then confirm that they don't come back. Many are the people who have been assumed dead for years, until the belated discovery that they simply left town without warning, moved to some distant corner of the Earth, and not let anybody know where they were. They are just absences, really; and my father, who has been an absence in my life for more years than I care to count, is an even greater absence, in that he doesn't even leave behind a hole. He is just a different shade of gone.

His death is still a fairly safe assumption, given his age and lifestyle and his poor state of health. On my last visit he'd coughed more than I'd ever seen him cough before, and in our infrequent encounters in years past he'd already coughed so much that you wondered why his lungs hadn't already resigned in protest. His departure, if death, is less a shock than a consummation long-promised, only unexpected in the sense that when it arrives, it is not something I had spent much time thinking about.

We only know he's gone because of a service I'd signed him up for, back when we were making more of an effort to stay in touch. Its sole activity was to call his phone daily just to confirm that he was still capable of answering. He had pronounced this a royal pain in the ass but agreed to it, primarily because I begged him. The calls had to be mid to late afternoon to guarantee an answer. Noon would have been too early, because it took him a couple of hours of dragging himself around before he was able to face even the limited challenges of his life; the early evening too late because he was a sleepy drunk and so completely anaesthetized himself by dinnertime that he could not be trusted to respond to even the most insistent callers. Once we established the effective window, he answered the call without fail until he didn't, and even then, the monitoring service tried two more times before sending the police. They found no sign of him and remained on the premises for three hours just to make sure he would not pop back in. Only after a week or so of further attempts was he presumed gone for good. It was possible, I supposed, that he wasn't. It was not unheard of, in the old days, for him to take a quick impulsive flight to some resort where he could lose a couple of thousand at cards. But there's a feeling you get when you're sure, and I was sure that gone he was. Transitioned into the thing that he had always learned he'd someday become: a maggot.

He had never offered any other details of that life to come, so I cannot say any more about it.

I strongly doubt that there is anything of value to retrieve, but Analise insists that I seek closure, and so we go to his house together, sweeping aside the empties on the front porch and gagging anew once making it inside. The foul air is so thick that I imagine it retaining its shape with the walls gone, a ghost-house of gray vapor to mark the place where once an embittered, alcoholic old man padded about, working on a life that had become an exercise in retaining a constant buzz. Analise opens windows to the east and west to create a cross-breeze, and sets the fans to going to disturb the murk; and over the next four hours we empty overflowing ashtrays, boxed porn magazines, and toss out most of the family photos. The refrigerator contains milk so ancient that it has partially solidified, cheese that has taken on the consistency of cardboard, and a Chinese take-out carton with half a serving of something so far beyond its sell-by date that it may have been what sent him to his future life as maggot; may have even been, judging by some of the bad meat in a barely functional freezer, an actual conscious attempt to evoke that future existence, with a similar diet. I don't know. I find one personal item I keep, a picture of Mom, though when I get home I will have to spray it with deodorizer to lessen its tobacco reek enough to bear having it around. I see another item I tell Analise to throw out, a picture of Dan that I stare at for a while, not with grief or nostalgia, but with the horrific whimsy of Dan's virus self infecting something and my father's maggot self infesting the corpse. *And then,* the thought comes, *the remains make their way to the sea, and nourishes the life that your crustacean self feeds on.* I have to go outside and be ill.

Analise comes out while I am still throwing up. "Do you want to leave?"

For one lunatic moment, I do not know whether she was referencing this house or this planet.

I could say yes, I'm dizzy, I need to go. But closure doesn't come that simply. I say that it's just the stink in there and that I'll be okay in a minute. She goes back inside to get some water from the tap, and until she returns I wish that I could disappear right now, even if only for a few seconds, even if only to see my future crustacean self safely recovered from its war and back in a dream of peace.

· · · ·

Later, thinking in bed while Analise sleeps gently snoring beside me, I try to tell myself that I shouldn't worry about that battle on the beach, not too much. After all, can you imagine just how widely variant the brief random tastes of life as a human being must be, to those who come before us? Experiencing them from some prior life as an alien mole, you could find this strange alien thing known as a person dancing, or scrubbing floors; making love, or puking his guts out; enjoying the best meal of his life, or having the shit kicked out of him in an alley. Imagine as your sole preview of human existence some adventurer hang-gliding, thousands of feet above a checkerboard landscape, feeling that delicious mixture of elation and fear and guiding himself toward a landing field he will not even reach for another five minutes? To the mole, it is hard to fathom that for the creature he barely understands, the pictured experience is not typical, even if it's regularly repeated. Now imagine that mole getting the same human being, only this time he's waiting on some line at the post office, early December, and experiencing only the overpowering need to pee and the hope that this interminable vigil doesn't last another hour. These are two snapshots from the life of one person, and so are snapshots of myself kissing Analise as we both lean on the deck of a ship, and me holding Analise as she shudders through the aftermath of the discovery that she can never have children. So are me laughing with adolescent hilarity on a roller coaster and me sitting under a bridge less than a year later, knowing that my shitty father will beat me if he's still awake when I get home.

My crustacean exults in the warmth of the sand beneath it, and also wars with natural enemies across a beach wracked with carnage? That's a minor discrepancy by comparison, compared with the one that separates my ebullience upon finding out that Analise loved me, and my later brief burning hatred for her, when I found out from her tearful confession that she'd spent the past year of our married lives making secret rendezvouses with a succession of men.

Explain that to the mole. She couldn't even explain it to me.

She just said that she'd gone a little crazy after her dreams of motherhood died, that she'd come to think that this life was just the purgatory she had to endure, while awaiting her genuine life as golden ape; and she had remembered in particular her sense that the apes loved each other with a passion that dwarfed anything felt like human beings. The vignette of herself and some male of her species going at it high above the forest floor had been simple and it had been pure. It had been everything. And she had found herself longing for it as alternative to our own complicated, sweaty, fumbling act, that act not without pleasure that was nevertheless the best human beings could manage. And so she had found herself a website catering to the one percent of people who reported that species in their future, and started meeting up with some of the men, and it had been a series of anonymous acts in motel rooms, and though the ghost of those future golden ape memories had been behind them, they had somehow never lived up to her visions of her post-human future, or even to what we had. "It was a compulsion," she said, and I hated her,

and I hated her for almost two years, and can you imagine the mole trying to understand that? Of course, the mole could not, any more than
this future crustacean can.

We can only say that this is part of a life we do not live ourselves,
temporarily bleeding back through time to infect the pleasures of this
one. And there's nothing that can be done about it, not that or a brother
who committed a fast suicide and a father who committed a slow one.

I only wish for another near-brush with death, so I can place that
future life back in context, and I want it to be only a brush, so I can do
the same with this one.

• • • •

Weeks pass. I suffer no further slippages. I am overcome with the painful visitation of hope. I begin to believe that my aneurism healed itself.
At my next visit, I ask Dr. Patel if this is possible and he orders various
scans, and when they are done he says what he had of course already
suspected: that my condition does continue to progress, even if it has
by sheer chance become asymptomatic of late. He even tells me, "You're
probably just entering the last peaceful interval before the end. It happens, for some lucky ones."

"What should I do?"

"Enjoy life. It's life. It's the last bit you'll get of this one, before you
go crustacean."

I think on this, and when Analise picks me up in the lobby, I suggest
something that I haven't for a while: that we book a weekend somewhere.
Not sometime next month, not later this month, but now. Leaving this
afternoon.

She agrees and we run home to pack, one small valise apiece. We
get in the car and we drive, hitting the road before we even decide on
a destination. When we finally pick one, navigation requires a U-Turn.
We think the U-Turn is silly and we laugh like idiots as the map updates.
How silly we are! How much like golden apes! And that doesn't even
make me sour, the way references to golden apes sometimes do, now.
With so little time to play with, I have come around to the philosophy
that my wife just had a lot of love in her and that I was never shorted in
it, not even once; and certainly not now. She is, I realize, just an alien,
operating from an alien set of rules, as she would be even if she did not
have memories of a golden ape future to motivate her; I am a different
alien, and so I operate under yet another, and this is normal, and it would
be foolish to pollute what little time I have left with grudges that we have

settled long ago. I am content. And we are headed for a bed and breakfast where we have stayed twice before, once before we were married and once afterward; a cozy little place with only ten guest rooms and a great view of the water. It is a place we should go again, when I will soon be gone; a place I will miss, for however long I live, as human being and crustacean.

* * * *

It is later. We have checked into our quaint little room, changed our clothes to something nice and strolled up to a narrow two-lane road to a little, strangely isolated little restaurant where I had salmon en croute and she had lobster tails with drawn lemon-butter. It briefly occurs to me to make a joke about her ordering something crustacean, but it's darkness I don't want to bring to the table. For the moment, there is no death here, just a man and a woman, enjoying a conversation of no substance, smiling at one another over wine and candlelight.

She excuses herself once, and while she's gone I flicker for a moment, returning to a world where my fellow diners are averting their eyes. I smile to let everybody know it's no big deal, and pick up my spoon; but inside, I am wondering. The glimpse I just received had nothing to do with being any kind of crustacean. It barely had anything to do with geometry as I understand it. Things . . . *overlapped*, though that's not the right word . . . with other things. I got what I got not out of any variety of sight or sound, but from other senses entirely; things that still buzz in my head, afterward. Whatever I experienced was the viewpoint of something so different, so alien, so removed from both the crustacean life I'd expected and the human life that still has a hold on me that I cannot provide even a single word of referent. I only know that I liked it. I don't know whether I've changed destinations or have simply gotten a glimpse of another destination, further on, and on musing about it for a second or two, decide that it doesn't matter. It will happen, sooner or later. I can worry about it when it comes.

So we dine and we have some sweet wine and afterward we return down that same two-lane road to the bed and breakfast. We intend to make love, something we haven't done for a while because of my fragile condition, but we are not ready for that yet because we are stuffed and she is the slightest bit tipsy. So we bypass our lodgings entirely in favor of a walk on the beach. We are not the only couple that has had this idea. There are two or three others, widely scattered, smoking or cuddling or adding to their own states of inebriation. It is dark and the stars are out, uncounted thousands of them, some of which may bear planets that are now home to people I've known, some of which Analise and I might travel to someday, perhaps even some of them where, by literally astronomical chance, we might meet again. At this moment, anything seems possible.

The two of us kick off our shoes and stand where the ripples wash over our toes, so we can knead the wet sand, and neither one of us says anything until she squeezes my hand and I tell her something she already knows, that I love her. She says that she loves me too and suggests that she return to the room for a bath towel, so we can sit on the sand for a while. I say that's a good idea, and let her go, promising to be here when she gets back, a promise that is silly, that has always been silly, because it is the kind of thing that nobody can ever guarantee, even in the prime of health. But I will do my best.

And then she is gone and I am left standing on the boundary between two worlds, the ocean and the land, thinking about nothing but that, until I spot something at the corner of my eye, scuttling across the sand.

Of course it's a crab, about half the size of my fist, that has somehow decided that my visit to its domain is hostile. It is not anything like the future self I imagine to be massive, though I have no real way of determining its scale, any more than Analise can determine scale for her golden apes, who for all we on Earth know might be microscopic. Its physiognomy is nothing like the creature I know I will someday be, or might for that matter be only five seconds from now; if I collapse to the sand, disappear, and leave Analise with no way of knowing whether I died here without warning, or instead gave in to suicidal impulse and marched into the water. (But then there are people in sight, also enjoying the cool night air, and they would see me go, either way, and tell her.) This crab possesses some of my future self's spirit, and though I outweigh it by a factor of one hundred, nevertheless seems to believe it could win a battle with me. Who knows? If the winner is the one who draws blood, maybe it could. And if it is anything like the future crustacean self whose life I have previewed, maybe it hears that hum that has so fascinated me: its music, which can mean anything.

As I gaze down at it, it raises its pincers in warning, and I have absolutely no doubt that it could cause me pain, another thing it happens to have in common with the crustacean self whose appearance in my future is now in doubt. Still, I regard the little creature benevolently. It is not my enemy, and I am not its, not even as an occasional consumer of seafood. Right now, and maybe for all time, we are brothers.

I gaze down in love and say, "Enjoy your trip."

EROS PRATFALLED:
OR, ADRIFT IN TIME AND SPACE WITH LASAGNA AND MARY STEENBURGEN

Ellis Neider met his soulmate. The End.

That's his story. The rest is annotation. We would almost skip that part, were it not for the stone knowledge that any love story not about masturbation does require at least two characters. The object of his affection does deserve something approaching equal time.

Ellis was a guy. Some men are guys, other men are dudes. Ellis was a guy. As a child, he was a little guy. As an adult, he was a bigger guy. Like most guys, he gave off the vibe that he knew the universe operated by a certain set of rules and that he had somehow missed getting on line when the powers handed out the books. He was not a bad guy. He was just a guy.

He had sandy hair that resisted combing, a problem that in the normal march of things would solve itself with the onset of male pattern baldness. He had a jawline that was always gray with incipient beard no matter how cruelly he applied the razor, eyes that watered if anybody stared at them for too long, and a wistful expression that went along with knowing exactly who his soulmate was and how difficult it was going to be to arrange the meeting.

You would like Ellis. You would likely be attracted to him, as potential friend if not as potential mate.

Ellis worked in a home supplies superstore. His specialty was cabinetry. He knew everything there was to know about cabinetry. This was not the area of expertise he would have chosen for himself as a child—he wanted to be an astronaut, in no small part because he knew about his soulmate even then—but cabinetry was what he did to keep body and soul together, a part of his life that amounted to the hours he spent waiting for them to be over so he could go on to the rest of his existence, which alas also consisted of waiting.

He had an Xbox. He blasted zombies. Sometimes he ordered pizza, a weekly habit that contributed to the slight bulge in his midsection. He wasn't fat, but he did not have washboard abs either. This is one of the factors that contributed to him being a guy.

He liked sci-fi. He didn't call it science fiction, but sci-fi. Again, this is of necessary interest in light of the secret connection he had to his soulmate. It would be critical to his eventual fate that he was a reader, one of the last among a dying breed, and that he preferred escapism to finely wrought tales of angst and character; essentially, anything where the hero roared rips, anything where the guy at the center of the action got to battle vast waves of alien vermin armed with nothing but determination and a sharp sword. His ideal of fiction was anything that made him cry *Yee-ha*. This was also critical to his fate, as if he hadn't encountered a certain model he wouldn't have ever had the opportunity to bond with the soul the cosmos had designated as forever entwined with his: the one he ached for, and was eager to meet, from the very moment he was aware of himself as more than an infantile ball of need, wailing for mother's milk. Before he could speak, his spirit had pierced the distance separating him from the one being whose spirit resonated most with his, whose heart beat in time with his.

And therein lay the problem.

His soulmate could have been a green-eyed, red-haired Irish girl named Caitlyn, actually fresh from the island with an accent to match, also with a ready smile and an infectious laugh, who loved dogs, classical music, and long walks in the woods; who played the guitar often but not well, who liked to sing but had no illusions of ever making a professional go of it, who just liked to warble on long car rides and in the shower because it made her feel good; who preferred t-shirts to blouses but could rock a sequined gown like nobody's business; who ate waffles every Sunday morning.

His soulmate could have been a brown-eyed, shaven-headed black guy named Rafael, born in Encino, who smiled little because he had a habit of brooding but could occasionally light up the room with his blinding white teeth; who absolutely loathed dogs but who maintained seawater aquariums, who liked hip-hop and loathed the woods but loved the beach, who had an odd passion for medieval German history and whose preferred form of wit was the pun; whipcord-thin, the kind of guy made to wear three-piece suits; who wore a jaunty trilby; who never ate breakfast, but was a bit of a bore on the subject of sushi and on the very long weekend he had spent trapped in Tulsa.

Ellis's soulmate could have been any one among billions of others.

Hell, in the absence of a soulmate, a good match, a person who could have been his best friend, a compatible sexual partner, a considerate roommate, a contributor to the family coffers, anybody not a total asshole, would have been doable, in multiple senses of the word.

And Ellis tried. Oh, he tried. He tried with Caitlyn and it was lovely, but there were times when his mind was on the unattainable other soul he knew, and she saw it, and after a few months there inevitably came the day when he went in for a dutiful kiss and she placed both her delicate palms on his chest and looked up at him with an affection millions of men would have crawled across shattered glass for and said, *We need to talk; clearly, I'm not the one.* He tried with Rafael and it too was lovely, but again there were times when his heart beat in time with that other unavailable to him, and there came the day when Rafael peered at him from across their king-sized bed and said, *You know what? This ain't working.* He tried with others, including a couple of Heathers and a Lucas and for a while with a Minerva, an actual Minerva, who had begun life as Menachem and who loved him, for a while, from across the greatest age gap of his sexual life, thirty-seven years. Minerva was gray but lively and for the longest time, the very longest time, she was not just lover but spiritual and erotic teacher, imparting a knowledge of life and the act that made Ellis a terrific short-term lover, but failed to render him desirable as life partner.

More than one person said to him, "Who the hell are you waiting for, anyway?"

And that was the thing.

Ellis *knew.*

He just thought it was impossible, and as crazy as you probably would.

First of the problems was that his soulmate was dead, and had in fact been dead for a long time.

Familiarity with romantic fantasies of various sorts have accustomed you to the premise that this can be overcome. In the pop culture realm you inhabit, people are forever finding their soulmates in eras far removed from their own. You may remember Claire Randall or Richard Collier or Kyle Reese or James T. Kirk, all of whom met their dearest love at times removed from their own. Then there was Doc Brown and a version of H.G. Wells, both of whom rode their respective time machines to lasting relationships with women played by Mary Steenburgen. Honestly, if you believe the advertising, a hottie from the Napoleonic Era isn't all that prohibitive a meet-up. That Ellis's soulmate had been dead of old age for much longer—approximately seventeen hundred years—would not have presented much of a problem by this precedent.

Nor do you expect much of a problem with the announcement that the soulmate in question was a non-human, living on an alien world. Again, you have seen guys making it with blue women and green women, women making it with furry guys and robot guys and lots and lots and *lots* of vampires. It happens. Love is love, right?

Here we introduce Ellis's soulmate.

At this point, we find ourselves obliged to introduce new pronouns. The creature in question had evolved in an entirely different ecosystem and the dance of time had created a trio of gender that did not line up with our classical two or any existing combination or variation, recognized or not. For reference we will use ze as the article and zer as the possessive. Zer name was unpronounceable by us, as the language zer species had developed reflected an entirely different vocal apparatus and frequent clouds of purple pheromone. Rather than make up a fanciful name to go with all that alienness, like Arailasi or Glar or Bathanibe or B'lg'n'z'p'th, we take pity and insert a name that ze would find as hard to fathom as we find some of those. Because human gender is irrelevant we could easily pick a male name, a female name, or a neutral name, but we will pick the name that best conjures zer personality: Myrna.

Myrna obeyed no biological model we know, but description is no insoluble problem. Ze was invertebrate, roughly oblong in shape, and semi-liquid, a word that sounds gross until you reflect that the same is true of you and me. Ze is best pictured as a stack of rubbery, flexible mats, containing all zer necessary organs and separated by a matching series of more liquid layers retaining heat, that constantly oozed out around the edges. The most accessible metaphor in your experience is probably lasagna.

Like the rest of zer species, Myrna was capable of locomotion and ze oozed about a planetary surface thick with the primordial juice, ingesting it at one end and excreting it at the other. Ze was charming and witty and a historian devoted to the study of an ancient war fought over an issue that would require an entire shelf of text to explain, of which ze was zer kind's most renowned scholar. Ze was considered a catch and ze had a series of assignations with zer own equivalents of Caitlyn and Rafael, both separately and together, and with colonies of melded creatures we would have trouble positing as conglomerations of Phils and Aimees and Vitos and Yukios. You need to know that if you did the heroic labor necessary to translate everything ze did into human metaphor, ze would be the shy but dazzling creature nursing a white wine beside the fern, allowing the party to come to zer; ze had no personal need to do any chasing. Everybody wondered why ze hadn't settled down.

The answer was that, from the moment ze first congealed from the elements that gave zer kind form, ze knew that zer heart—well, not actually zer heart, because ze didn't have one, but an organ of equivalent importance—belonged to a distant being of unaccountable strangeness, named Ellis Neider, who specialized in an arcane skill involving artifacts known as cabinets.

It was an uncanny connection, one that sometimes left Myrna doubting zer sanity, but it could not be denied. Destiny could not be denied. This Ellis, whatever he was, wherever he was, whatever nature of world had spawned him, was zer soulmate, and though ze made every conscientious effort to live within the dictates of zer biosphere, it was impossible to form any lasting relationships for as long as he remained zer destiny.

Ze pined over him all the thirty snumpoks of zer life, a not inconsiderable period of time among zer kind. Ze felt the tenor of his being, tasted his lust for life, his aching vulnerability, the million and a half ways his totality resonated with zers. Ze knew that it could never be, that he lived—actually, would live, as he was many years from being born—on a planet shocking in its conditions, infested by a race stunning in its venality and short-sightedness, in whose company he was trapped. Ze ached to join him, or to have him join zer, though common sense counseled that this was impossible.

Ze wept, or performed the equivalent of weeping, which is more we're not going to go into.

If only—

*   *   *   *

—*If only.*

Allowing for the many years it took the light of Myrna's world to shine in the night sky above the apartment where Ellis had spent the latest in a long series of evenings alone, after yet another paramour had fled to parts unknown after sadly telling him that permanence was not in their shared future, Ellis thought these same words with what was as close as the universe allowed for synchronicity.

He stood in his apartment, so recently vacated by his last consolation prize of a lover. He gazed upon the art prints on the walls, and the oversized flatscreen on which he and that individual already fading in his memory watched their last date night movie, *Love, Actually.* The tears would not come. But he did feel the familiar yawning void in his heart, and he thought of the being he did not, personally, think of as Myrna. He knew that ze was alien, and he knew how crazy his mother would get if he ever explained to that poor, fluttery woman who kept hinting about grandchildren that this was the match every atom of his being insisted on holding out for. He wondered what ze was doing, and the answer of course was that on zer world so many generations had passed that all zer substance had been passed on to the other living things in zer own planet's cycle of life; allowing true synchronicity, ze was in a million different places, being eaten, metabolized, breathed in, exhaled, excreted, or otherwise churned the way we are all fated to be, once our own substance returns to the soil. It may be true that zer own soul was being similarly recycled, its bits and pieces distributed among the other beings of zer world, but these are philosophical matters we need not go into now. Forget the actual gulf of time. Allow the signal passed between two beating hearts, or between one heart and whatever ze had, to stand in simultaneity. At what passed for this moment, no two lovers had ever yearned more desperately for their very first meeting.

Ellis had no reason to believe that tonight was any more fateful than any other night, nor was there anybody present functioning as the equivalent of the officiant of a Passover seder to explain exactly why. He just thought his poor excuse for a life had been shattered to empty pieces again. And so he stormed about for a bit, fulminating, cursing his fate, scaring the cat, drowning his sorrows in a belt, and after a timeless time spent performing the various other manifestations of his pity for himself, indeed a period that might have lasted days, did what we all do in such a circumstance and began to move on. He sighed and reached for another consolation, which at this fateful moment was a very old and battered science fiction novel that he had bought years earlier but that he had always neglected in favor of more contemporary works. It happened to be the first to fall within the reach of his grasping hand, at this instant when—again, allowing for the chronological lag—Myrna was just as vehemently yearning for him.

Because he picked up that one specific book, he in very short order read Edgar Rice Burroughs's rationale for John Carter's first trip to Mars.

As I stood thus meditating, I turned my gaze from the landscape to the heavens where the myriad stars formed a gorgeous and fitting canopy for the wonders of the earthly scene. My attention was quickly riveted by a large red star close to the distant horizon. As I gazed upon it I felt a spell of overpowering fascination—it was Mars, the god of war, and for me, the fighting man, it had always held the power of irresistible enchantment. As I gazed at it on that far-gone night it seemed to call across the unthinkable void to lure me to it, to draw me as the lodestone attracts a particle of iron.

And with that, the fictional gentleman from Virginia conveniently found himself on Mars, where he was to meet his soulmate, the lovely Dejah Thoris.

Perhaps on any other night, Ellis would have retained too much grounding in the concrete world of his everyday existence to make the leap of faith. But right now, he was bereft; right now, there was nothing to his four walls and IKEA furnishings to hold him. Right now, he could feel zer, the being who would complete him, calling. Moving like a man in a dream, he left his apartment and descended the stairs and stood in the street outside, looking up at a sky that was for this moment brilliant in its clarity and its abundance of starlight. One bright light among all the thousands seemed to him to pulse with an urgency that dwarfed all its brethren, and this one he addressed with a degree of focus he had never known, through which he sensed the creature who was the focus of all his longing, addressing zer own stars with just as much fervency.

The universe bent itself to their shared will.

He was transported out of his clothing, which remained on the pavement, the only forensic evidence in a mystery that the world of his birth would never solve. Those who knew him, his family and friends and co-workers and the lovers who had drifted away in sadness, would spend the rest of their lives wondering what had happened to good old Ellis, that poor guy who really did deserve happiness, even if he never had seemed to figure out what he wanted.

Ellis felt nothing but an interval of dizzying speed, stars going by so quickly that he perceived them as Doppler-shifted streaks, and then—

• • • •

He found himself standing on a moist glistening crag in an ill-smelling murk, in a literally unearthly cold beneath stars that, for all his knowledge of astronomy, could have been those of Rio, or Shanghai, or Cleveland. It was cold enough for his breath to emerge as vapor, which made the disappearance of his clothing especially unfortunate. Goose bumps erupted, but this was not just a function of the cold. He could sense zer nearby, and more importantly could sense zer registering him, and through their connection felt a boundless joy that was echoed by his own. Whatever the differences in their species, whatever the differences in their cultures, this was a moment that was always meant to happen, and that meant their differences would be met, and overcome, the two hearts, or again his heart and whatever it was ze had, finally joined in one.

The world seemed empty. In one direction, there was nothing but an endless plain, marked here and there with greasy streaks that glistened in the starlight. In the other was a wall so high that it scraped the very heavens, so wide that there was no possibility of walking around it, so featureless that there was no possibility of even an experienced free climber, which he was not, to scale it. Wherever ze was—and he could sense that ze was near, aware of his proximity but as unable to spot him as he was to spot zer—it seemed that the task of crossing this last divide would need to be zers. He had no doubt that ze would. This was zer world. If there was a gap in that towering edifice, ze was the one who'd know where it was.

And then the entire wall rolled forward, making the earth—or whatever you called the surface of a planet that was not Earth—shake. He fell to his knees, saw the clearly biological ways in which the layers of flesh undulated, perceived the yawing wave action in the more liquid layers that separated them, and understood for the very first time that the many barriers between himself and his one true love had never been limited to time and space and biology. All of those could have been overcome. More critical was that which was about to crush him, in a manner more literal than the repeated crushings his heart had endured over the years. Given half a chance, their love could have transcended time and space and biology. It had never stood a chance of surviving the one difference that turned out to be way more critical than any of those: Scale.

For Ellis it was like being run over by a horizontal avalanche. He was flattened, liquefied, rendered a stain that, because of the vagaries of his body chemistry's interaction with that of this alien place, would never rub off. He ended his existence as zer tattoo.

So yes, for him, that was the story, the one we began with.

Ellis met his soulmate. The End. An object lesson in holding out for what's perfect, in defiance of what probably would have been perfectly nice.

For Myrna it went a little differently. Upon reducing him to a thin crunchy paste, ze perceived his sudden absence but not the nature of his departure, and though ze was distraught for a while, adjusted. Within four turnings ze was part of a triad. It was for zer a union short on passion but high on practicality, and there were nights when the mating was quite nice, where ze managed to get all the way to what zer kind considered climax without once resorting to fantasies of zer alien Ellis, or forlorn conjectures over what had ever happened to him. It was a happy ending, or at least a contented one, and we can take comfort in the awareness that they had both gotten what they always wanted, even though he was the only one who had even a heartbeat to be fully aware of it.

Ze, on the other hand, would always think of him as the one who got away, much as we happen to know that he really didn't.

THE THING ABOUT SHAPES TO COME

Monica's new baby was like a lot of new babies these days in that she was born a cube. She had no external or internal sexual organs, or for that matter organs of any kind, being just a warm solid filled with protoplasm. But she was, genetically at least, a girl, and one who resembled her mother as much as any cube possibly could. That wasn't much in that she had no eyes, no nose, no mouth, no chin, no hair, nothing that could be charitably called a face or bodily features, not even any orifices larger than pores. But she had inherited Monica's healthy appetite. Placed in a dish in a puddle of Monica's breast milk, she throbbed in deep appreciation and absorbed it all in a matter of minutes, becoming as plump and as satiated as a sponge. As far as anybody could tell, she was a happy and healthy cube.

It had been a difficult birth, given all the corners involved. Labor had been the biological equivalent of trying to fit a square peg in a round hole. But there was no reason, they said, to worry about her health; her constitution was strong, and there was no reason to believe she couldn't live a long, comfortable, and healthy life, devoid of any serious problems unrelated to the general inconvenience of going through life shaped like a cube. The presence of nerve impulses even confirmed that the child could think, while providing little in the way of speculation over what she could possibly have to think about. Look at her the right way and it was even possible to consider her beautiful, in that she was smooth on all her planes, sharply defined on her edges and corners, not off by so much as a millimeter, in any of her vital measurements. This wasn't the kind of beauty Monica had envisioned when she'd hoped for a beautiful child, but there was a starkness to her daughter's lines, a mathematical purity to her, that made it impossible to want to use terms like *disfigured* or *deformed.*

Monica had hoped for an old-fashioned baby, of the kind that had been common when she was a child, the kind with the rounded features and drooly toothless smile and the foreshortened arms and legs and even—yes, she'd looked forward to this as well—the end that would need to be wiped clean and powdered on a regular basis. She had wanted a child who would someday delight her by calling her "Mama," and one day rise on uncertain feet to toddle off and force her to give chase. That would have been the ideal. But she had also known that these days the odds of ending up with a baby that looked like that were about one in a hundred thousand, and dropping. More and more women were giving birth to cylinders and pyramids and crosses and rhombuses, with the vast majority of the newest generation emerging as playful spheres. Of all the young mothers Monica knew, only one had been blessed with a baby shaped like a baby; and that mother seemed genuinely haunted as she pushed the infant around in its pram, aware that the world was watching, feeling surrounded on all sides by legions of frustrated kidnappers and pederasts. The mothers of children-shaped children had to take care to shield their progeny from such predators, because the number of predators remained constant even as the number of possible targets for their vile intentions now described an asymptotic curve that approached but never quite reached zero. Most of the young parents Monica knew were lucky enough to have been blessed with spheres that could roll around and bounce into one another and even learn to descend household stairs, though rarely to ascend them. A sphere, Monica thought, would have been a fine alternative to a traditional baby. A sphere she could have taken to the park and played with. But complaining about that was like spitting in the face of God. Certainly, a cube must have other talents, other good points to love.

Of course, Monica's mom and dad were upset, not just because their teenaged daughter had given birth to a cube but also, unspoken, because that cube's mocha-brown coloring suggested that, since Monica was white, the unknown father must have been black. Dad wore an unmistakable scowl as he held the new arrival in his hands, his rheumy eyes a million miles away as he bid a mental farewell to any future birthdays involving tricycles and baseball gloves, or even dollhouses or drum batons. He weighed the cube in his hands, wondering aloud whether he was holding her upside down or right side up, or if there was any way he could tell that she even knew she was being held. He said, *Maybe we could put a label on it, to let us know which way is up.* Monica's mom was even less subtle, complaining: *She's square.* A doctor corrected her at once, saying, *No, Mrs. Hufready, she's not a square, a square would be flat. She's a cube.* Mom was slow to absorb the correction and demanded, *What the hell is my daughter going to do with a square kid?* It was impossible to hear Mom's tone of voice and not know that she would always fail to get it, that even if she came around to loving her granddaughter for the beautiful, geometrical solid she was, she would still be slow to pick up the etymological differences, using the offensive s-slur for years to come without ever quite understanding why it was wrong.

As for herself, Monica felt the tug of maternal love the second her child was placed in her hands, and rotated so she could see that her baby was indeed the same on all sides. She was a member of the younger generation, the one that had grown up in the age of such births, the one who had been prepared to gestate and nurture a darling shape of her own. She saw in her daughter's being, her substance, the oneness of her, a divine spark that all of her dreams of a more conventional child could not deny. She felt the pit of bottomless responsibility open wide before her and, with no reservations, leaped in. Asked for a name to put on the birth certificate, she told the doctors, "Her name's Di."

* * * *

Di was a well-behaved child, who lay in her crib and regarded the world around her with a calm acceptance that never crossed the line into brattiness or fussing for the sake of fussing. She didn't cry, but from time to time she hummed. This was always a sign that it was time to feed her. She was an angel whenever food was provided, sitting in the center of any puddle laid out for her and plumping visibly as she absorbed it. She also thrummed in the presence of her mother, though rarely so in the presence of her grandparents, whose generational instincts had somehow failed to kick in, and who most often referred to the baby as "that thing." Monica did whatever she could to jump start their hearts, but that seemed a losing battle, and she spent more and more time retreating from them, taking Di into her own bedroom and doing all the maternal things she was required to do in private, where they would not be a source of constant irritation.

Aside from that, there was no shame. Monica felt no compunction about taking Di out to the park, where there were only a couple of lonely "normal" children who looked furtive and uncomfortable in the playgrounds littered with mostly immobile shapes other parents had brought and placed about the rusting swing sets and jungle gyms, in the hopes that the environment would provide the kinetic opportunities that the limited motive ability their own offspring lacked. The most popular item of equipment among the parents seemed to be the sandbox, where the pyramids, cubes, and rhombuses, arranged in rows and left to interact in any way they could, resembled the half-buried buildings of some desert city, assaulted by the aftermath of a sandstorm. A couple of times Monica placed Di there, among the other edifices in the miniature boulevard, until she noticed that when playtime was over the parents didn't always leave with the same kids they'd come with, and excused away any accidents of identification with the excuse that they were just too hard to tell apart.

Some conscientious parents made more of an effort to personalize— as in, "render a person"—their shape-children. Sometimes, Monica sat beside one determined young woman who dressed her pyramidal boy, Roger, in jean overalls that buttoned midway up his converging slopes, held in place by suspenders that hooked around his single vertex. The outfit came complete with plush-toy, fake legs dangling from his base. The effect wasn't very convincing, not even with the cartoonish smiley-face drawn on one of Roger's three risers, a representation of two dot eyes and bubblegum pink cheeks curving into a happy mouth that, on Roger, resembled disrespectful graffiti more than an actual personification of a child. Even when Monica forced herself to entertain the premise, she couldn't help noticing that the simulated head came to a point, which to her mind made Roger look feeble-minded. To be sure, Roger's mother had tried to ameliorate that point with a scruffy little wig and baseball cap, but how much more noble, she thought, was his actual shape, shorn of pretense? It was primal; it was classical. It was the shape of monuments, of constructs that lived forever. The pyramid-in-boy-suit was, by comparison, just a transparent ploy, a stab at imagined normalcy that emerged as grubby and pathetic by comparison. Monica could only glance at her own Di, who embodied self-contained perfection so well that she looked the same from every angle, and tried in vain to summon the mindset that would have led her to subject the darling to indignities of the same sort that Roger's mother subjected on him. It seemed deluded, anti-maternal, and likely hurtful.

Other times Monica wandered over to the fenced-in area where the spheres played. It had been a basketball court, though the poles and hoops had been taken down, and the game being played by about two dozen spheres of different sizes resembled nothing that had ever been played between teams. Unlike cubes, which were stable once placed in any given position and could be trusted to remain where they were put until somebody came by to move them, spheres were pure chaos, harder to stop than to start, an explosion of play potential that manifested as a collection of runaway ids. They rolled about at high speeds, some describing predictable orbits and others changing their course according to the whim of each passing moment. They collided. They bounced. They slowed, pretended to rest, and then accelerated like streaks of light, as if fired by invisible cannons. It was impossible to tell if they were actually playing with one another, or, as it seemed to Monica, *at* one another. Perhaps they perceived their fellow spheres as annoying obstructions and not as fellow inhabitants of the universe. But there was an energy to their play, a potential that reminded Monica of atoms colliding with one another, searching for others with which they could combine and form strange new substances, with none of the properties of the original contributors. But when Monica put Di down in the center of all that splendid chaos, just to see what would happen, the answer was nothing; her child just sat in the center of it all, unstirred, a closed system.

◦ ◦ ◦ ◦

When Di was two, the world experienced a slight upswing in instances of what were by then called traditional pregnancies. It wasn't much. It didn't amount to more than about five thousand more than the population had been told to expect. But the furor over this development vastly exceeded its statistical significance. The news media questioned: Is the "plague" over? Had mankind been saved from this strange mutation?

In a few short months further numbers would come in, and the answer to both questions would turn out to be no. This was nothing more than a statistical fluke, the kind of phenomenon that only happens because the numbers come up that way; no more significant that the occasional odd family that, in the old days, would produce ten boys in a row without a single female face among them, without much affecting the fifty/fifty ratio in the general population. When things evened out, the vast majority of young mothers continued to pump out spheres and cubes and pyramids and rhombuses, and the line on the graph that reflected the percentage of pregnancies that resulted in baby-shaped babies continued to descend, inexorably, toward zero.

But while the illusion lasted, many people seized on the premature intimations of hope to initiate debates over what to do with what they considered a lost generation. Shape-children were abandoned, thrown out, offered up for adoption. Many mothers were pressured by loved ones to admit that the things they'd carried in their bodies, expelled, and cared for, were, not people, but things unworthy of their love that could now be discarded.

Monica's parents were among the people who took this position. They pointed out that she had not held down a job, or done anything else with her life, since Di's birth. They said that all she did was feed "it" and care for "it" and talk to "it" as if "it" could hear her. They told her that she showed even more devotion than a "regular" mother, but that it was a devotion poured down a black hole that swallowed far more than it could ever return. *It's a parasite,* they told her. She argued that it had always been possible to see babies as parasites feeding off the generation that birthed them; for a while, at least, they contributed nothing but smiles and coos while demanding food, attention, and energy. How, she wanted to know, was Di different? This somehow never closed the argument but rather brought it back to the beginning, to the declaration that Di had done nothing in her short life but increase in size and in her need for nutrients. *You don't like the word "parasite"?* her parents asked her, *Try "vegetable."* The point was that Di still showed no sign of ever being able to interact with others in any meaningful way. There was no reason Monica had to continue paying the price of being devoted to her, not when there were "places" that could take care of Di just as well as she could.

This was not just a single conversation. Or perhaps it was, if you can say that a series of conversations, continued over days and weeks with only short interruptions for sleep and the necessary business of being alive, was a conversation. There was no halt to it. Monica took it with calm, and then with anger, then with long bitter silences, and then with weakness: *Yes,* she said, *Of course, I'm not saying I agree, but I'll look at one of those places, already.*

And so they went to a facility for abandoned cubes. It wasn't called that. It was called a juvenile home. But it was only open to cubes, specializing in that particular shape and no other, to the point of specifying in its charter that any children whose parents submitted applications would be carefully measured before acceptance, to ensure that none of them had sides that differed in proportion by even a stray millimeter. As Di thrummed contentedly in Monica's lap, the administrator, a woman who seemed inordinately configured out of ninety-degree angles herself, explained that "fitting in" here was not a social concern but a physical one. The children were stored on shelves in stacks of three, and any whose dimensions were at all disproportionate caused dangerous instability among those stacked on top of them. But—she smiled—there was no reason to believe that this would be a problem with Di, who was just lovely. In her case the examination would be, doubtlessly, no more than a formality.

Monica and her parents took the grand tour, and by now were not surprised that the place was, very much literally, a place for warehousing unwanted children. The shelves stretched twelve feet above a cold concrete floor and the length of a football field into gloom, each stacked five high with cubes of sizes ranging from newborn to adolescent, the latter being so large they could have contained old-fashioned console televisions. A sprinkler hose moved down one of the aisles on a track, spraying them with a liquid that, the administrator advised Monica, had been formulated to fit all of their nutritional needs. Another spraying light mist washed them off. Stereo speakers played gentle instrumentals while the cubes thrummed, staying in tune. Dust motes danced in the cold, dim light. Monica's father asked the administrator if they had a system in place for knowing which child was which, and she pointed out a placard at the end of each row, which detailed the number range of those stored on each shelf (as in "1200- 1503"). The names, she said, were backed up weekly and stored off-site, for convenience, but they didn't really matter all that much, as these were not children who would ever come when called.

The silence and seeming acquiescence of Monica and her parents encouraged the administrator to ramble. She told them about the most memorable mishap the facility had ever suffered, a case where none of the attendants had noticed that the cube on top of the stack had experienced a growth spurt faster than those of the cubes it rested on, and a cascade occurred that had toppled first that stack and then the other stacks next to it, resulting in a pile of thrumming objects who may have been unhurt but who presented a challenge that didn't often come up when dealing with other children, in that they were faceless and identical. It had taken a flurry of DNA tests, undertaken at great expense, to determine which child was which, not that anyone at the facility felt it especially mattered.

Monica asked permission to place Di on one of the shelves, just as an experiment. The administrator beamed and told her to go right ahead. She placed Di on an empty spot, murmured that there was no need to worry because Mommy would be right back, and backed away, stopping only when she was ten feet away, and then again when she was twenty, and finally again at fifty. Di was hard to pick out among all the other cubes. She was indistinguishable from the others her size. But Monica thought of all the times she had been in public places like busy streets or stadiums and auditoriums, looking out upon crowds of hundreds or even thousands—the way all of those faces, as unique as they may have been as Joe, or Sue, or Brad, or Laura, had been reduced by the sheer number to shifting pixels, making up a grand mural whose only identity was that of the mob. It wasn't easy to pick out any one person in that place either, because they were all alike, becoming something different from all the others only when they were approached and examined for the cues that made them individuals. She wondered if anybody working at this warehouse ever picked up one of the cubes and felt its warmth against their own. But mostly, she wondered how many of them were screaming.

· · · ·

The spheres rebelled the year Di turned fifteen. By that time it had been years since Monica had been able to hold her only child in her lap, or cradle her in her arms. Now Di was the size of a dishwasher and could no longer be moved except with a hand truck; at the speed she was growing, it would soon be impossible to move her from Monica's little studio apartment except by knocking down one of the walls. She was by far the most prominent item of de facto furniture in a place that otherwise knew little more than a kitchenette, a convertible couch, and a second-hand television.

Monica, who since cutting off all contact with her parents had worked two jobs to maintain the place, remained as attentive a mother as she could be under the circumstances. She made a point of eating breakfast with Di every morning; Di absorbing the contents of a sponge saturated in shape chow, Monica using Di's ceiling-oriented face as the dining table she otherwise didn't have room for. Di was, if nothing else, a considerate person to eat a meal on. She absorbed spills, and to Monica's maternal eyes seemed to be particularly fond of coffee.

Monica still spoke to Di all the time, telling her that she was special, assuring her that she was loved. There was no way for Monica to know that her child heard or appreciated any of it, and though she held on to her faith with a ferocity that her few friends considered heroic if not deluded, those doubts sometimes overwhelmed her, leading to sleepless nights and a sense of all her life's energy being poured down a black hole.

The little studio became a fortress when the spheres rebelled, many millions of them at once, a revolution declared at the same moment in a hundred major cities around the world, though it was hard to say what grievances they thought they had, or what cause they might have championed, other than anarchy. Thousands, of all ages, from newborns to near-adults, rolled down the Spanish steps in Rome, thousands more down the zigzag planes of Lombard Street in San Francisco, uncounted numbers rebounding at high altitudes from glass skyscraper to glass skyscraper in Tokyo in what amounted to the most horrifying Pachinko game ever played. Cities with steep hills were the most vulnerable, of course, but they were not above tailoring their acts of terror to the local possibilities: Witness what they did in Saint Louis, where hundreds of them herded shrieking innocents through the Gateway Arch and back, scoring goals.

In the city where Monica lived, they just broke things, smashing through automobile windshields, overturned trucks, and made it their solemn duty to pay a visit to every single china shop in the greater metropolitan area. She spent that long night huddled in her studio, assuring Di that everything would be all right as the sounds of fear and destruction rattled her windows. She lost herself in bleak thoughts of the price that would need to be paid for all this, the price that would no doubt be levied against innocents like Di, who could not wage war against anybody. Spheres, she thought savagely, were troublemakers by design. They could spin; therefore, they were revolutionary. It was not just their privilege but their nature to take the path of least resistance, no matter what lay ahead of them. It was just the way they rolled. But cubes, like Di? They were solid, dependable, and uncomplaining. They received love and asked for nothing more. How terrible it was, that they would now be lumped into the same category as such delinquents.

But in the morning, the sounds of destruction gave way to an eerie silence that persisted until the sun reached its height in the sky. Monica ventured downstairs alone and discovered what those who had already left their homes already knew: that whatever had driven the spheres to their destructive madness the night before seemed to have exhausted, not just their rage, but their will to live. Wherever she looked, in every direction, the spheres remained in the places they had come to rest, moving only when some of the people they had terrorized kicked them against walls or beat them with golf clubs and bats. Some, damaged by their fury of the night before, had lost so much of their bounce that they responded to any fall from a height not with an exuberant spring but rather with a sullen and indifferent thud. As she walked the city, she saw workers clearing their unresisting forms from the streets and loading them into trucks; and she knew that, all over the world, all those not claimed by loyal parents would be taken somewhere far from sight where they could be stacked in pyramids or plowed into canyons or otherwise forgotten about. For the first time in a life spent taking it as matter of faith that her cube had a soul, she found herself doubting that all shape-children did, and wondering if they would even care about being discarded in this manner. But what was the alternative? Tolerating what they'd done? Leaving them where they'd landed and trusting that they'd never run roughshod over the landscape again? It was not that she had no answer. It was that every answer she had made her feel dirty. It was a warm day but she hugged herself, shivering from a cold that originated somewhere deep in her marrow.

Before she returned to her apartment to check on Di, she stopped by the riverfront, where some of the smaller spheres had landed. Hundreds, ranging in size from golf ball to weather balloon, had landed in the water and were floating downstream toward the sea, where she supposed their next adventure would be serving as the playthings of dolphins. She supposed it as fitting a fate as any.

After a while Monica picked up one of the tiny ones that had landed on the shore, which, judging by its size, could not have been more than six months old. She spoke to it, asking if it could say anything to her that would help her to help them, or at the very least, explain just what, in any of their short lives, had embittered them so much that they had to turn to violence. Naturally it didn't answer. She asked if there was anything it could tell her that could help her understand her own daughter, who was so close to being too large to live at home. Again, it didn't answer. Tears sprung to her eyes and she cried, *At least you could move! At least you could have an adventure!* But no reply was forthcoming and in a fit of rage and resentment she tossed the infant into the river, somehow unsurprised when it didn't land with a single splash but instead skipped over the waves, landing here and there but between those moments of impact remaining in flight, like something defiant and free.

* * * *

Nine months later, the very last shape-child—a random squiggle, like a strip of twisted macaroni—was born in Jakarta. Baby-shaped babies filled the Earth again. It's worth noting that nobody ever came up with any reasonable scientific or theological explanation for the nearly two decades that saw such a drastic change in Mankind's reproductive output; nor did it seem all that important, as long as it never happened again. Explanations are perhaps best left to the philosophers, who persist in seeking meaning even for those of life's mysteries that remain random, or pointless, or so subtle in their inner workings that examining them is as destructive to the wonder itself as scattering the components of a pocket watch.

For all of us, meaning arrives in installments. It might be actual and it might be wishful thinking. We can only report the facts and hope that they provide closure.

To wit:

Many years later, a rented car drives across the desert, taking a unmarked exit off the paved road to a dirt trail that carries its lone driver past some low hills to a hidden valley on the other side. Trailing a cloud of dust like a comet trail, it passes a little-used gate and descends into a vast caldera that, from a distance, looks like a recent settlement constructed in haste, with prefabricated buildings. It is in fact one of many around the world. Sprinklers water the immobile cubes, spheres, and squiggles, making rainbows in the air that, left to its own design, would be dusty and arid.

The car parks in a place that has been marked off for that purpose and out of it emerges a silver-haired, but still energetic, woman, squinting at the harsh desert sun. She looks out upon the survivors of a generation, the biggest of which are now three times her own height but which remain as voiceless and without affect as they ever were. Donning a pair of mirrored sunglasses, she sighs and makes her way down to the orderly paths past a very small number of other visitors, finally reaching a certain cube among many, that she has visited so many times she could probably find it in her sleep. No one other than her could see anything about this particular shape, which now towers over her like a monument, that could possibly distinguish it from all the others in its row or the rows that bracket it. But she smiles sadly when she sees it. To her, the shape before her has an individual character different from all the others. It is a person.

To be sure, Di also shows some of the ravages of time. The side facing east shows some sun-damage, and a swath of the side facing north shows some bad discoloration left over from the last time she needed to be sand-blasted for graffiti. But she thrums as always in the presence of her mother, who places a single wrinkled hand against her side and speaks words very much like those she's uttered on any number of other visits. We do not need to know exactly what the silver-haired woman says. We can likely already imagine it, and reconstruct its meaning if not the actual words. What she says is not clever and it is not significant, and it will never appear in any book. But it fulfills its purpose, breaking the silence and ameliorating the harshness of the desert air.

Eventually, though, it's time for the visit to end. The silver-haired woman whispers a few final words, lets her right hand brush the side of the vast shape before her, and turns to leave. Always, before, she never turned back. But today something—perhaps maternal instinct, or perhaps a voice that only she can hear—makes her turn before she has traversed twenty paces. And this time she sees something in her strange daughter that she has never witnessed before: an alteration in the nearest of her previously, featureless faces. It's a rectangular opening, seven feet tall and three feet wide, extending upward from the patch of dirt that has become Di's permanent home.

The silver-haired woman returns to what she has no trouble recognizing as a doorway, and runs her fingers up and down the jamb, filled with wonder at its sudden appearance. She turns away from it and peers up and down the path between the other children of her daughter's generation, to make certain that nobody is watching. As it happens, nobody is. Di has chosen the perfect moment. This gesture is only meant for one.

The silver-haired woman cannot see anything past the opening but darkness, not even when she removes her sunglasses and shades her eyes from the glare. The precise nature of the answers to be found inside are not available to her, not out here. But she senses no threat: just the welcome the young are supposed to extend to the old, when the most inexorable of life's many passages transfers the responsibility from one to the other.

With another glance up and down the row, just to be sure that she remains unobserved, the silver-haired woman murmurs the first words she has ever been able to speak in response to an act Di has committed out of personal volition. "All right," she says. "Good girl."

Then she takes the first step, and her daughter lets her in.

MANY HAPPY RETURNS

Gorman was on foot, crossing a frozen continent. It was not Antarctica. That was light years away, and so over. Nobody went there anymore. This continent he had chosen for his latest adventure was bigger, broader, colder, deadlier, nastier. It was not fun. Every step was an occasion for regret. He was probably going to die. He was glad he came.

Subjected to howling winds and sub-freezing temperatures and deprivations capable of making a Shackleton want to lie down and die, Gorman lost four toes and forty kilos, which sounds a little bit like I'm saying he's lost ten kilos with each toe, an unintended implication since no one's toes have never been quite that large.

He was starving, is what that sentence meant.

Today he was resting his hopes for immediate survival on ice fishing. After hours of back-breaking effort, he succeeded in carving a hole in the frigid surface through which he could dimly see the black waters of a vast inland sea; and he lowered a thread painstakingly unraveled from his thermal pants and braided to some semblance of tensile strength, the end tied to a hook piercing one of those blackened and severed toes, into that unknowable darkness, hoping that whatever came to investigate it would swallow whole and not nibble. Then that sudden strong jerk came, promising sustenance. Alas, it was such a strong jerk that it almost pulled him into the hole after it, and only his own strength, still prodigious despite being drained by the conditions, enabled him to wrestle whatever it was, first giving it the slack it needed to struggle, then pulling harder, digging his cleated boots into the harsh ice so he could draw the beast farther, and farther, out of the darkness and into the light. It was only when the ice started to crack all around him, in a perfect circle, that he knew he had landed a leviathan, and he was just beginning to contemplate whether survival would be best served by following his instincts as a hunter in search of a meal or those of potential prey hoping to avoid becoming one, when he became aware of

a limping robot
ambling toward him
from the east.

There was no telling how long it had spent crossing the ice field while Gorman was distracted.

It was a slender, golden thing, dinged here and there from a service lifetime of being smashed with heavy objects. Approximately the shape and dimensions of a human being, it honored that model with its body language, even though all it had for a face was the thin little crease on the bottom quarter of its cylindrical head that functioned as a workable smile. It carried a small rectangular object, and though Gorman already knew what it was, there came a point in the robot's approach when sight and not experience identified it as a sealed green envelope bearing the phrase *Happy Birthday*.

The robot stopped before him and said, "Happy birthday, Gorman."

Gorman said, "Fuck off."

The robot spun on its heels and retreated toward the jagged peaks on the horizon.

* * * *

Later, in a dying place where the air stank of soot and where the shadows were darker than could be accounted for by the mere poverty of light, Gorman dragged himself across a dusty wooden floor and into a room littered with wreckage and the gnawed bones of uncounted others who had sought this refuge before him.

In the last few minutes he had been wounded in his right leg, which was useless, hence the requirement of using his other leg to propel himself, on his back, into this place where, his exhaustion and blood loss suggested, he would now be making his last stand. He bore a pulse rifle across his chest, burning his bare chest through overuse, and he knew that it really did need a cooling cycle before being used again, if he didn't want to risk a phase-out that would incinerate him, his shambling pursuers, and all other physical matter within fifty meters. But an entire horde of the bastards was swarming into the ruin after him and it wasn't like he had much of choice. Even as the top of his head encountered an obstruction, some fixed piece of furniture too heavy to be shoved aside, one of the damned things stuck its rotting face past the threshold and forced Gorman to devote yet another short, controlled burst to the cause. Elsewhere in the crumbling house, that is, elsewhere but still too close, far too close to allow Gorman satisfaction at taking yet another of the bastards down, its companions heard the sound of the rifle's signature *zzzzzzizzzzzzit* and started coming to investigate, which really made this a fine time for

the golden robot, which sported a few more dings and dents acquired since its last intrusion

to come striding through the same threshold,

still bearing the sealed green envelope reading *Happy Birthday.*

It said, "Happy birthday, Gorman."

Gorman said, "Fuck off."

The robot exited, turning the corner just before the same opening became dominated by worm-ridden, gnashing faces.

· · · ·

Gorman scaled the thousand-meter edifice of the sultan and infiltrated the seraglio, home of three thousand stunning courtesans with nothing to do but dream of the next time their lord returned from his travels to the borderlands of the empire, and regale each other with the stories they had heard of the one man, the rogue of legend, the grand adventurer, who it was said could satisfy even these ladies trained all their lives at the arts of pleasure, who could show them for the first time ever what it meant to not just give, but also to receive.

O, just to contemplate him, though even a man that storied could not possibly get past the city walls, and even if he did, could not evade the crack legions patrolling the cobblestoned streets alert for the very first appearance of a man his description, and even if he did, could not possibly defeat the brutal swordsmanship of Azir the Endless who forever guarded the base of the tower, and if he managed that trick, could not possibly retain enough stamina to make the climb, and even if he did, could not possibly do more than collapse in a heap, pencil moustache and all, when he finally entered the silky and perfumed spaces within; could not possibly have anything left to offer the silky and perfumed spaces within *that*, not without a good long rest, he couldn't. But yet here he was, his bare chest glistening with sweat, his ardor undeterred, about to say the words that all the tower's residents, the most divine creatures in all the world, had waited all their neglected lives to hear—

The robot

entered through a veil of silk

carrying a green envelope bearing the legend *Happy Birthday*

and said, "Happy birthday, Gorman."

Gorman replied, "Fuck *Off.*"

This time with *special* vehemence.

And the robot, knowing that this one might have been pushing the issue,

fled.

• • • •

Robots are persistent. It is their chief attribute. Given directives, they keep doing the same thing until instructed otherwise, or falling immobile due to wear. This robot showed wear but not exhaustion; it could be delayed, but not deterred. It kept showing up, exactly once per situation, still bearing that green envelope, which, though it looked like it was made of brightly colored paper, was actually the same substance as its own somewhat dented but overall indestructible self. It always brought the same green envelope and always said, "Happy Birthday, Gorman," and Gorman kept telling it to fuck off, and it kept going away for a little while and coming back a little while later, always in significantly altered circumstances, always with the same result. It did not care. Its feelings were not hurt. It was a robot. It had long since resigned itself to an existence in the same tradition of mimeographs and outboard motors and lawnmowers and home computers, which is to say that despite being unappreciated it would keep trying to do its job for as long as it could, only to be to harangued with colorful profanity by the user. It would have felt neglected if it had received any other reply. It saw the replies it did receive as love. It appreciated Gorman's persistence even if he did not appreciate its own. This, too, was its nature.

Meanwhile, in its spare time, it composed novels. It had in its brain twenty volumes of an epic generational saga set on the Mongolian Steppes. If ever submitted to a publisher, the books would have been recognized as the product of a true literary titan. This could not happen until its current task, delivering its birthday card, was completed. We won't even talk about its symphonies or its never-tested innovations with pizza dough. We could, though. *Molto bene.* It had a lot on the ball, this robot. It honestly did. But first things first.

· · · ·

Gorman stood atop the highest spire in a desert teeming with upright stone pillars, thousands of meters high. There were many more than an army of cartographers could count, all aligned with perfect precision, like the grave markers at an armed forces cemetery; whatever angle he faced, he could see a perfect line of them, extending so far into the distance that the ones on the horizon congealed into a undifferentiated brown blur.

Gorman had no doubt that there was some sensible rationale for their existence but hadn't done the research, assuming only that it could not have been the natural forces of erosion. He wore a wingsuit, rippling in the high-altitude winds, and more than once in the last five minutes or so he had almost found himself hurled into the orange skies by a sudden powerful gust.

His ambition here was simple. The pillar on which he stood, the tallest out of this vast multitude, was the starting position of a flight path that, if accomplished with critical precision, would hurl him through a narrow cave that had formed in the tower about two hundred meters away; that is, if he didn't miscalculate his angle or fail to course-correct for any turbulence and instead flatten himself against its stone walls, perhaps even before entering the cave that offered only a few centimeters of clearance on each side.

Assuming he accomplished this feat, risky to the point of suicidal even for the most accomplished wingsuit users, he would then find himself hurtling toward another opening, somewhat tighter, in another pillar a couple of hundred meters beyond that; and assuming he managed this trick, he would face another, and then another, and another, all requiring many split-second micro-adjustments to navigate, if he didn't want to end his storied existence as fresh paint.

In short, he was looking forward to threading himself through not one and not two, but twenty-four separate little openings, all while traveling at terminal velocity, and any unexpected air pocket or downdraft an exercise in illustrating with the human body the result of using a trebuchet to fire a watermelon at El Capitan.

The odds were against him, but if he accomplished this, he would be a wingsuit legend for all time. He licked his upper lip, tasting sweat, because this wasn't the easiest thing to just up and do

and behind him

still limping,

still carrying that green envelope,

the robot said, "Happy birthday, Gorman."

What came next was, in precise medical terminology, a conniption.

Gorman said, "Will you just *please* just leave me alone, for once?"

And it was the first time he had phrased it that particular way, because the robot cocked its cylindrical head and said, "What, precisely, do you mean by *for once*?"

· · · ·

By mutual agreement, they went to talk it over.

There was a world known as Hezipicalezaranigablanis, not to be confused with the much more frequently visited Hezipicalenzanigabladis, a place that has many of the same features and which many devotees of galactic travel prefer for its low-salt cuisine.

There the most beloved spot was a café overlooking the lava fields with their glowing, multi-colored, delicious-smelling swirls of molten rock, guided by unseen intelligences into spectacular fractals.

The entrees were expensive, but they did this Death by Chocolate thing that was downright sinful, that was considered an absolute must, especially if you have a guest, at which point you were really required to request two forks.

Gorman and the robot sat at a little table with a candle burning in a little jar between them, him glowering, the robot humming. It wasn't absently recalling a tune. It just hummed now, from some inner deterioration difficult to quantify. It held one of the two forks provided by the waiter and had even partaken of a bite, even though robots are not supposed to eat; chemical analysis of exotic substances happened to be one of its capabilities, and the Death By Chocolate certainly qualified. At the moment the rich mouthful left its fork, the hum briefly became an mmmm. "You can have the rest," it said, placing its fork back on the plate. Gorman just glared at it. He hadn't taken a taste yet himself, which accounted for at least part of the glare, even though he was profoundly irritated at the robot and would have been glaring at it anyway.

He said, "Precisely what would it take to get you to leave me alone?"

The robot said, "I have one assigned task. Delivering your birthday card."

"It is not my birthday."

"It is only not your birthday because you have not yet accepted the card."

"I don't want the card."

"It's a very nice card," the robot said. "There's a joke set up on the front that pays off beautifully on the inside. The act of opening it pulls on a tab beneath the card stock and makes a little cartoon puppy slide diagonally across the interior, simulating exuberant play. The implication is this creature, a King Charles spaniel, is happy to see you on your special day. The presentation is really more appropriate for an eight-year-old but is designed to appeal to twee individuals of all ages. There are some handwritten thoughts under the words '*Happy Birthday,*' expressing deep affection by people who care about you. As an experience, it's over in less than two seconds, but if accepted as a gesture of intended sentiment, it is timeless, a good thing since all the loved ones responsible for sending it have long since crumbled into dust."

"I don't care."

"I'm just a robot, but this strikes me as awfully callous of you."

"It doesn't matter," Gorman said. "The family agreed to let me have a year off after graduation."

"It's been more than a year. All your relatives are dead. Entire civilizations have fallen, even if your family's financial holdings have not."

Gorman offered the nastiest of all possible smiles. "Don't force me to explain it again."

The robot did not need him to explain it again.

Because Gorman had explained it, anew, every single time he'd agreed to sit down for a civilized discussion: the arrangement he had put in play, in an agreement that would remain in play until he, himself, decided otherwise. It was ludicrous, but it was ironclad.

I, Aloysius Gorman, assert my right to a one-year sabbatical. During that year my financial interests will be handled by a blind trust, from which I may draw at will to fund recreational activities of my choosing. I shall continue to enjoy all the benefits due me as a member of my family, including all available medical and rejuvenation services, for that year. I herewith certify that when the year is up, I shall agree to assume my hereditary position as head of all family enterprises, and devote all my efforts to the preservation of our fortunes and the perpetuation of the family dynasty, which I understand shall require permanent sequestration at our ancestral estate on Lithigigilaparanagavisinu Prime. One year from now, I will open my birthday card or eat my birthday cake and commence adult life. Until then, no one associated with the family shall attempt to place any restrictions on my activities whatsoever. Signed, Lefty.

This had been his nickname since an unfortunate childhood encounter with a trained bear. They'd grown him a new hand, but the sobriquet had stuck. And since Gorman had done everything that had been required of him, in all the family covenants, up to that moment, nobody had suffered even the slightest qualm about letting the kid go off and get the whole idea of fun out of his system. Even though they knew he absolutely loathed the Family Estate, fifteen thousand gray rooms without a single window or wall decoration: a place designed to deprive whoever currently maintained the family fortune of a single possible form of recreation. Play, the theory went, is play. But work is serious business. And work never ends. Surely, everybody thought, by promising to return after only one year, when so many prior heirs had negotiated for as many as twenty, Gorman had demonstrated a keen understanding of his responsibilities!

Surely, they thought, ignoring the key provision in one of the contract's forty-two footnotes, the one attached to the word "year."

In the absence of any conscious decision by the principal to end this sabbatical early, the period referenced as "year" shall be measured by the standard astronomical definition of a galactic year, and the principal's birthday shall be defined as the twenty-four hours immediately following the completion on that year.

Everybody just assumed that the boilerplate *galactic year* referenced the calendar most commonly used throughout human civilization: which was to say, the 365 days of approximately twenty-four hours apiece, established on the home world.

How surprised they were to find out that the astronomical definition referenced the length of time it took the sun of humanity's original solar system to orbit the entire Milky Way galaxy, a period of very approximately *two hundred and thirty million* years.

He could do this for effectively forever.

Which would effectively require the robot to do the same.

The Robot said, "It really is very good cake. Just look how rich and chocolatey it is. Mmmmm."

Gorman replied, "You're really not fooling anyone, you know."

* * * *

Gorman went off to the running of the brachiosaurs. The planet that sponsored it had bred them for speed and malice. They were aware of the scurrying little people in their path and they stomped with gusto. Some of the stains would never come out of the pavement. Gorman emerged alive but with but the back of his shirt stained by the guy who had come in second place. It was, he declared, fun.

Meanwhile, the robot went to a bar.

Robots had bars. Why wouldn't they? The word was derived from the Czech word for laborer. Laborers get off work and go to bars. Robots assumed all the functions of laborers. Hence, robots had bars. Robots were capable of wanting to get drunk every once in a while, or at least of simulating that function as they simulated most other human functions. From time to time, between tasks, they went to the taverns that accommodated them and they played darts, argued over sports, picked up other robots over the pool table, got sloppily sentimental over the good old days, and hollered that they could whup the tin backside of any other bucket of bolts in the house. Every once in a while, they became belligerent and took pliers to each other.

And they had drinking buddies.

Gorman's robot sat in a rear booth beneath a stained-glass window of red and green diamonds and poured out its troubles to its posse of sympathetic ears, only a couple of whom actually had ears. One was a war-droid with immense grip strength for mangling the enemy. Another was a sex worker with immense grip strength for other purposes, and yes, this had led to unfortunate confusion more than once. A third had been designed to provide lonely people with companionship and had one function, nodding. A fourth, PHP-321, specialized in attending funerals. The four of them listened at great length while Gorman's robot waxed maudlin about its seemingly eternal lot, and when the tale was done emitted various beeps and whistles of deep camaraderie before uttering various values of, "Yeah, but whaddayagonnado?"

The war-droid advocated beating the living crap out of Gorman, the sex worker advocated a certain brothel where all the workers had been designed to combust following orgasm, the provider of companionship nodded, and PHP-321 said there was as yet insufficient data for a meaningful answer.

None of this was at all helpful. None of it had, to date, ever been helpful.

Gorman's robot sighed—because machinery is capable of sighing, as anybody who has ever heard the air brakes on a city bus can tell you—and said, "You know the stupid thing? I honestly don't blame the son of a bitch flesh puppet. The family fortune really is self-sustaining, and with the mechanisms in place really will continue to flourish indefinitely without him. What need it has of a human steward died out millennia ago. The family only continued to require one's residency in that colorless mausoleum because of its traditional, and long-since antiquated, misconception about adulthood being inconsistent with whimsy, about seriousness between inconsistent with fun. It's only persisted this long because they want somebody to look dour and unhappy in the oil paintings. If I had the ability to defy my programming, I would say the hell with it, myself, and congratulate him on the brilliant loophole he's provided himself. Certainly, my sympathies are with him."

The war-droid advocated beating the living crap out of Gorman, the sex worker advocated a certain brothel where all the workers had been designed to combust following orgasm, the provider of companionship nodded, and PHP-321 said there was as yet insufficient data for a meaningful answer.

"And yet," Gorman's robot said, "in providing himself with freedom, he has trapped me in an infinite loop, one that prevents me from seeking some more appropriate destiny for myself. Honestly, guys. I'm at a loss. Help me."

PHP-321 ventured that there was as yet insufficient data for a meaningful answer.

This was a key reason why none of the other robots liked him much. He was so invested in the identity politics of robothood that he never relaxed.

⁕ ⁕ ⁕ ⁕

Gorman built a house of cards the size of a continent. It involved over forty million decks and took centuries of engineering. He saved the aces of spades for the turrets. He was in the midst of placing the last card when the robot stepped up behind him and said, "Happy birthday, Gorman."

Gorman retreated to a monastery on the planet Xiurithapolythicostari. His penance included self-flagellation and the penning of young-adult novels about a kid who has no problems, who suffers no setbacks, who experiences no adventures and is delivered no epiphanies during the course of the entire twenty volume series. The kid pretty much went to school and came back. Gorman was penning the last chapter when the robot appeared behind him and said, "Happy birthday, Gorman."

Gorman decided to enter the world of organized crime. Using bribery and guile, he cornered the interstellar market on a substance necessary for the lubrication of the hinges in the doors to starship toilets. It was a fantastically valuable material because on starships ordinary grease won't do; the special conditions in hyperspace has a nasty habit of rendering it sentient, and there's nothing in the universe more attitudinal than smartass grease. His vast criminal empire eventually constituted forty-two systems. Came the day when he was eating in an Italian restaurant, facing the front door, when the robot defied the way the interruption of mobster meals always seem to go by emerging from *deeper* in the building. His greeting of "Happy birthday, Gorman" started a crossfire and subsequent gang war that ended civilization and home food delivery throughout the sector.

And so it went.

Almost a million years passed. It's hard to say how close the interval came to a million years exactly. Maybe it was within a few millennia. Maybe it was within a few months. Maybe if Gorman had waited another thirty seconds, an invisible gong would have rung, in whatever hypothetical room measures such things, and the critical event would have occurred on the precise anniversary, to the nanosecond. It wouldn't have mattered, but certainly it would have been cool.

In the interim, Gorman had lived and died every possibility but boredom. He had been crushed, immolated, devoured by ants, appointed king of monarchies that like to behead their kings, infected by diseases that make the eyeballs swell to fifty times their original size, starved to death, frozen to death, criticized to death, immortalized in statues, watched those statues crumble, had those statues injected into his veins, suffered fever dreams, written them down, been praised for his surreal poetry, and been suffocated beneath the fallen huge tower of publisher remainders. He had lived lifetimes in peaceful contemplation and in quiet desperation. He had done everything, been everywhere, man, and the infinite possibilities still stretched out before him, an unending buffet that he could never exhaust, not ever, even if there were days of recovery from radiation burns (or whatever) where he most sincerely wanted to.

Today he was investigating a new thrill game that had slaughtered entire populations of the galaxy's rich and stupid. It was a high-altitude dive, sans parachute or any other form of braking or steering mechanism, toward a range of mountains customized for that very purpose by canny sculptors. They were too steep to climb and too cold to survive, and there was no safe place, on any of their peaks, to land, even for someone with the tools necessary to arrange a soft landing. But someone who positioned his fall *just so* could parallel one of the sheer cliffs from a distance of centimeters, catch an updraft capable of slowing him just a tad from terminal velocity, ultimately come into contact with the ice cliff and slide downward on the wet layer, and thus be in contact with the mountain, but not actually crashing into it, as over a span of several thousand meters the cliff became a slope and the slope became a horizontal glacier, harmlessly spending all that angular momentum until the high-altitude diver came to a soft landing in a mound of nice, soft snow at the end of the field. If all that sounds crazy, that's because it was crazy. Any plunge one millimeter out of true, any change in wind velocity one kilometer per hour removed from prior calculations, any angle differential as minimal as a fraction of one percent, and any muscular twitch at all, at any point while the participant skimmed the ice face, and the factor that would need to be calculated by the very next diver to make the jump would be the red smear the prior one left behind. The pastime killed off ninety-nine point nine nine nine nine nine nine percent of all rich idiots who attempted it, one reason why the economy of the world that hosted it was entirely fueled by the syndication rights. People loved watching well-heeled schmucks acting like well-heeled schmucks, and especially dying like well-heeled schmucks.

But it had now come down to Gorman, standing on a tiny platform so high above the mountains far below that they looked like ripples on a giant white bedspread, and leaping, taking aim at a narrow target that he had to hit straight on, or die.

He jumped, and on his way down, the robot appeared in free fall beside him, still carrying that green envelope, and said,

"Happy birthday, Gorman."

Gorman said, "For God's sake. This has to end."

"You are a fraction of a degree off course."

Gorman made the miniscule adjustment, but didn't thank the robot; he had grown very alert over the ages, and was supremely aware that to say thank you even for an unrelated service might have been taken by some judicial authorities as a grateful acknowledgment of the birthday greeting, and this of course would never do. Instead, he said, "Look, this is pointless. In the unlikely event I make it to the end of a galactic year, a motion will be filed in any court still operating at that time, asserting that what I meant by galaxy was not the Milky Way but the entire nearby group of clusters, and that the year I referenced was their interminable orbit around some vast, incomprehensible something-or-other, not destined to end until the stars go cold. I'm telling you, I am better at this than you are. There is no point in persisting."

"I think there is," the robot replied.

"What possible rationale can you have for that?"

"Only this: the pattern common to so many of the distractions you've sought. Like the present example, they're all dangerous. Increasingly, they're all suicidal. Even the sensory pleasures, like that harem, are best defined as the prize awarded at the end of an effort overwhelmingly likely

to bring your destruction. I believe that this is no accident. I believe that
a man who seeks death before his next birthday is a man who prefers it
over life. I think that, beneath it all, you are tortured by guilt over aban-
doning your responsibilities."

"That's just stupid," Gorman said. "My responsibilities as the family
defined them were bullshit."

"Indeed they are, but they are still responsibilities, and you have still
employed bullshit on a cosmic scale to evade them, betraying all the traditions of your family in the process. I believe that while you imagined
you would escape without consequence, that you know that you have
not—and that nothing you have done to distract yourself, for all this
time, has ever fully succeeded in erasing the debt you secretly cannot help
but acknowledge. I think you even know by now that as the sole remaining survivor of your family, any choices you must make about how to live
your adulthood are up to you, and might not even resemble the fate you
escaped so long ago; that the terms of the family contract are no longer a
threat to you, and that if you continue to flee, it is adulthood itself that
you flee. I believe that this disconnect will continue to torment you, and
I believe that it will only get worse until you accept your birthday card or
eat your birthday cake and move on. This is a passage, Gorman. A passage all human beings must cross, that it is nevertheless my responsibility
to arrange."

Gorman was quiet for a long time, and then he said, "Damn you,
robot."

"That you have, yes. And I'm so sorry."

"I won't give in."

"I know. And so, here we are."

Gorman impacted the cliff. He was slightly off, but not fatally so; it
was a little bit like being hit in the ribs with a sledgehammer, and several
of them splintered, but after a moment of seeing all his lives flash before
his eyes in 3D Sensurround Percepto Smellovision, found that he had
indeed fallen into the groove that so many before him had failed. He slid
down the side of the mountain, slowing on schedule, braking on schedule, feeling the vertical surface beside him become a steep grade under
him and then a gentle grade below him, finally leveling out, whee, I
mean, seriously whee, though he started to spin a little as his momentum
carried him onto the deceleration plain, where the giant mound of snow
he was headed looked a little like another Himalayan-class peak, so grand
and magnificent it was.

Despite the ribs grinding together like toothpicks, despite that stupid tarnished and dented robot still following in his slipstream with that damned green envelope still clutched in its hand, despite everything, Gorman thought, despite everything, he had made all the right choices, and there it was, the symbol of every choice he had made, the snowbank, giant, fluffy, creamy, covered with lit candles, and for some reason it beggared his mind to contemplate, smelling even from here of vanilla frosting, with shavings of coconut.

Just before impact, the robot said, "Happy birthday, Gorman."

THE HOUR IN
<u>BETWEEN</u>

Oscar crept up on his sleeping wife and shattered her skull with five blows from a claw hammer.

The years might have robbed much of the strength from his legs and obliged him to do most of his walking these days with a cane, but his right arm was still almost as powerful as it had ever been. The first thundering impact struck Deanna with a crunch he could feel at the base of his spine.

There was still value in being sure, and so he raised the hammer again and brought it down a second time, burying much of its head in everything she had been: the toddler who had chased butterflies, the bride who had beamed in her wedding photos, the teacher who had taught English Comp for twenty years, the mother of one failed daughter and one merely defeated son, and finally the old woman who in her last years had precious little to say to her husband beyond businesslike reminders of whatever needed to be done around the house. He did not want her to linger, so he struck her the third, fourth, and fifth times, none of these three blows as accurate or as effective as the first two, but devastating enough between them to put out Deanna's right eye, and flatten her nose, and turn the crater he had made into a larger and wetter obscenity.

This, he understood once the deed was done. was the moment that would forever come to define him. Very soon, he would only be the man who, at the end, bludgeoned his sleeping wife before then joining her in death. It was only Deanna who'd be remembered in her fullness, Deanna whose passage through her last seconds would not become the image that defined her forever, but would instead be the sad footnote to a life well-lived.

As he'd always expected, nausea struck.

The room had been dim enough to protect Oscar from seeing everything his hammer did, and was now light enough to ensure a quick retreat to the master bath. Oscar hurried around the queen-sized bed, past the bookcase and bureau, and into the room he thought he needed.

For a second or two he thought he would not make it, but by the time he was ready to kneel by the toilet, the spasm had faded. The water in the bowl could remain unsullied.

He stopped at the sink to scrub his bloody hands and he almost got sick again when he flipped on the light. The face in the mirror was covered with a fine spray of red freckles, larger wet spots that looked like open wounds, and -- sticking to the side of his face like postage -- one shard of something that could only be chipped bone.

Washing his face was pointless. It would only get bloody again later, when he shot himself. But there were too many things still left to do, and the thought of continuing to do them while pieces of Deanna dried on his skin seemed beyond obscene. So he turned on the water and grabbed the hand soap, working up a powerful pink lather in water just hot enough to burn. Afterward he used one of the hand-towels to clean the bloody hand print at the light switch, and another to clean the floor and counter of any blood that had dripped off him in the length of time it had taken him to surrender to this last, pointless vanity. His pajama top, drenched with Deanna's blood, went in the basket. So did the soap, though he'd washed it clean too. This was pure consideration for his son, Richard. He didn't know what happened to basic toiletries when a house had to be cleaned up after a murder-suicide, but the thought of Richard, or some other member of his family, innocently washing up with the same bar that had soaked up Deanna's blood, struck Oscar as almost as loathsome as the killing itself. So he spared everybody that, at least.

A light moan escaped him when he turned on the bedroom lights and faced the aftermath of his crime. He'd already prepared himself to find Deanna's head reduced to an imploded bowl, and yes, that was pretty much as awful as expected. But he hadn't figured on all the blood he'd flung against the walls and ceiling with every upswing. The carved headboard was a spotty, dripping abstract. Her bedside lamp dripped pieces of her. The ceiling was a constellation of random red stars. The room where Oscar and his wife had slept for the last eight years, since the rising cost of retirement living had forced the two of them to sell the house he had never stopped considering their real home, had been marked in places he had never thought the murder could reach. There was even some marking the spines of the complete Dickens arrayed side by side on a shelf so far away from the bed that he could only marvel at how far blood could fly.

He hadn't expected the rising stench. Over and above the copper tang of blood were the more acrid smells of urine and feces, the last salvo of the final argument Deanna would ever have with him.

Oscar couldn't sit on her side of the bed. He did rest for a moment on his. If he had not had a few things still left to do he might have gotten the revolver and shot himself right then. But the moment seemed to require more in the way of last words, perhaps an apology or epitaph. He could not come up with one. What rushed to fill that empty space, in the absence of any legitimate eloquence, was a pair of before and after snapshots, one from the beginning of their marriage, and one to this its last night: in the first snapshot, a soft-focus close-up of the early post-honeymoon days when he and Deanna had made sweet love more often than not; the second snapshot the final exchange of every evening for more nights than he wanted to name, including this night's, Deanna waiting until he was safely under the covers to ask him whether he'd made sure the front door was locked, and not feeling fully safe until he got up to double-check.

That had become every night's last conversation, in this house. It had been their final conversation, period. *Did you lock the front door?* Yes. *Can you check?* Okay. There had never been any point in saying that he had already made sure before coming to bed. It was not real for her, not safe, until he got back up and trudged to the front door and rattled the knob. Yes, he would say, coming back, I checked. Unspoken in the exchange was confirmation that all dangers were now left outside; a sick joke, he thought now, given that she eventually lost her life to a husband who had always shared the fortress with her. Nor was that the only thing left unspoken. *Did you lock the front door?* Yes. *Can you check?* Yes. *Do you love me?* Unmentioned, not for so long that he could not remember the last time either one of them had uttered the words. Now she was gone and here he sat trying to come up with something else he could say, something that could possibly make a difference to a cooling sack of flesh that could neither accept, nor reject, his excuses.

No, there was no point in saying anything, now. There would be epitaphs later, from people who had the right to say something. Any words from him would be an abomination.

He returned to the bathroom, moistened a washcloth, and returned to her side just long enough to retrieve the favorite photograph which sat framed on her nightstand. Deanna had been the one who insisted on keeping this photograph, one of the only ones they still had of all four family members together. He had caught her sitting at the edge of the bed holding it from time to time, and had known it was not the younger version of herself she was looking at, not the younger version of her husband or the younger, happier version of Richard. She was lost in the image of Erin, captured in an instant long passed that Oscar had always known said nothing at all relevant about his only daughter.

The frame he didn't even bother to try cleaning. It was an overwrought silver thing, sculpted with ivy and French curves and so ornate in its determination to honor whatever image it surrounded that some of the blood that had descended into its fissures would be next to impossible to remove from there. But for Deanna, and for Richard, who might be taking this photo home afterward, Oscar could spare the few seconds it would take to wipe the glass. He used the washcloth to scrub at the blood spots, first thinning them and then clearing them away, until a day thirty years past was once again clear.

The photo captured four people standing in sunlight, against the blurred, but colorful outlines of an amusement park merry-go-round. The parents stood in back: Oscar, wearing black glasses and slight moustache of a type that the verdict of time had decided ugly. Deanna stood next to him, tilting her head, her slight overbite adorable in the way it had always been, back then. Their grins were forced, as both had been fighting killer tension headaches. Richard and Erin stood before them, smaller versions of their parents. Fourteen-year-old Richard's smile guarded in the way that it would somehow always turn out to be guarded, into well into his years as a man who could never free himself from the awareness that life could plunge him down a trap door at any moment. And Erin? Erin. Captured in a rare moment between screeching tantrums, between refusals to eat, between cutting herself and shoplifting and arrests for prostitution, before an adulthood that manifested as disappearing without word for years at a time, Erin here appeared as the platonic version of herself, her eyes bright, her smile uncomplicated, her warmth for the complete stranger the family had drafted as photographer so undiluted by her well of rage that it was possible, just from the image, to fall in love with her. Oscar would have liked to know that girl. He would have given an arm for a way to show her to the Erin he'd been obliged to raise, the Erin who might not still be alive for all he knew, and say, this, honey, this girl, this one here, that's who you were meant to be, and who you *should* have been.

The photo was one of those random moments of stopped time that tell the wrong story, that lie in the way that the wrong kind of grin can sometimes make the most exceptional paragon of humanity look, in that instant, like a creature depraved and evil. The actual day had been a nightmare. Nothing had made Erin happy. The rides were stupid. The food was disgusting. Her parents were awful. Her brother was gross. She didn't want to be there. For half an hour, no more, the sun had seemed to come out and she'd seemed willing to forget the bottomless loathing she had for them, for her brother, for herself, and for life, really. She had said she'd try to have a good time, and held on to that promise long enough for the photo to be taken. But only half an hour later she'd be a storm of resentment again.

There were precious few other photographs of Erin. She'd destroyed many of them in her early teens, retaliating against her parents for one punishment or another; and had after fifteen become such an impossible terror, a nightmare of uncontrollable anger and sudden violence that the impulse to commemorate the moment had somehow never come up. A lone fleeting photo of Erin at sixteen, sticking her tongue out at the camera, trying to evade the lens and thus reducing herself to a blur, was the most recent image Oscar and Jeanne had; there were none of her as an adult, as she would never allow any to be taken during any of her rare subsequent appearances. Oscar had stored away as many of the remaining pictures as he could. He didn't destroy them and had no problem with them continuing to lie stacked in boxes he never opened or in albums he never cracked, but for the most part didn't them hanging in plain sight, ambushing him at odd moments like evidence brandished by some angry prosecutor.

Deanna had insisted only on continuing to treasure this one. He had no idea why. But looking at the picture, really looking at it, Oscar was struck only by two things: one, that despite everything, Erin had been a very pretty girl, and two, that if she was in fact alive, it might be a very long time before word ever got to her about what had become of her parents. She might never find out. Or she might find out right away and storm into the funeral, to make it the same screeching atrocity she had made of everything else.

Either way, it was outside his power, and none of his business. That was the thing about death. It drew a curtain, made everything outside your own years a sequel that you would never be permitted to attend.

He stored the cleaned photograph in a drawer, protecting it from the spatter yet to come.

Tracking blood through the house but forcing himself to the knowledge that it really didn't matter much at this point, he went to the kitchen and poured himself a tall glass of ice water, from the dispenser on the refrigerator door. He drank that in a gulp and filled a second glass, to be nursed while he parked himself at the breakfast nook and peered out a window that, at this time of night, facing the woods the way it did, shielded from starlight the way it was, might as well have been painted black. It was a view he knew well, because he'd slept only fitfully in his old age and had made many post-midnight trips to this table and that view, finding in its very impenetrability an eloquence that spoke to him in ways that a more conventional landscape never could. Tonight, the view seemed even more illustrative. Nothingness, it was cleansed of everything that he would no longer see again: the glitter of sunlight on rippled water, birds cocking their heads at nearby sounds, leaves animated by errant breezes, clouds that looked like dogs, rainfall making ripples in tiny puddles, motionless frogs deciding for reasons of their own that it was time to head somewhere else.

Hell, forget the things he would never see again. The list of things he'd now done for the last time was even longer, and more primal. He'd never take another shower. He'd never read another book. He'd never issue another apology. He'd never eat another apple, never smell another flower. He'd never see another running child, never receive another kiss on the cheek, never squint at a bright light reflecting off another mirrored surface. He'd never encounter another appalling headline and would certainly never hear the words deficit, bipartisanship, gerrymandering, socialist, reactionary or global warming ever again.

The total number of steps he still had left to walk, once he rose from this table, were certainly less than one hundred and likely less than fifty.

Now, that was an interesting statistic. He felt some minor curiosity over the exact figure. He could count those final steps, if it mattered, crawl into bed for the last time aware at the end that his last mile had consisted of precisely thirty-two paces, or something like that. But no; such idle interests would serve him not at all, and were also therefore best forgotten.

His son, though.

His son remained.

Oscar returned to the refrigerator, filled his glass, and once again sat down at the breakfast nook, which was now forever just a nook because he'd eaten his last breakfast.

He had spent a lot of time, over the last few months of increasing resolve, debating just what kind of message he should leave for Richard. He had thought about writing a note, thinking about how a few words would never be enough and how pages on end would be far too much. He had put aside the idea of an apology and given up on ever providing a list specifying all the things that his final brutal act was not. *No, neither one of us was sick. No, I was not depressed. No, I did not act in anger. No, I did not hate her. No, life had not become too hard. No, I did not crave death; I just looked at the time that remained and saw that we were old and knew that every day still remaining to us it would less and less resemble anything worth living.*

Had Oscar been inclined to explain himself, he would have written something he'd learned early on: that life is a series of thefts, some small, some large, some gifts yanked away in moments of horrible trauma but most ferreted away in secret while you aren't paying attention. He would have written: our childhood sense of play goes away. The sense that everything's going to be all right goes away. The warm glow of youth goes away. Freedom from responsibility goes away, passion goes away, illusions go away, health goes away, potency goes away, the sense that life can still surprise you goes away, and so on, until you finally reach the point where you're left with nothing to do and four walls you know by heart.

He knew he didn't need to write this down because Richard already knew it. For as far back as Oscar could remember, Richard had faced life with a kind of resigned dread that stayed with him even as he did all the expected things, married and fathered children and been what other people would call a success, without ever shaking the melancholy that clung to him wherever he went. His joys had always been fleeting, his smiles those of a man shaking off an open wound. Oscar had never found his son really celebrating anything, not his graduations from high school and college, not his marriage to Delia, not his success in small business, and not even the coming of his own two children, without keeping some stored sadness in reserve. He was the one you spotted at family gatherings, in moments when he happened to be away from others, dropping his false face and revealing the trapped gaze of a trained animal, performing the expected tricks of adulthood without ever taking any special satisfaction in them. He was the one, sipping beer on the patio while he and his father watched the grandchildren bounce a ridiculous inflatable ball around, who had suddenly said, "They don't have a clue, do they? They two still think it's going to be fun."

Oscar had said, "You don't know. It might be."

Richard had shaken his head. "I don't remember the last time I had fun. I don't even remember the last time I wanted to have fun. I'm just acting out of habit. And part of me can't wait for it to be over."

Oscar remembered what it had like being the father who wished he had known some wise and knowing thing to say to that. He hadn't any. He'd wound up commiserating. In not so many words, but in laments that had lasted much of the afternoon: *I agree, son. I wish it was over, too.* The two had wound up sitting in silence warmed not at all by the nearby laughter of children, knowing each other better than they had ever wanted to, the chief connection between them that of men who had forgotten what their lives had ever been for. Richard didn't need a note. Richard would be living through enough of a nightmare over the next few days, and beyond, but he didn't need a note. He wouldn't take what his father had done as an enigma. He'd see it as grim confirmation: just more of life's true shape, revealing itself as its false fronts failed.

Richard only needed to be alerted so he could do what he'd always done, and just get on with it.

The breakfast nook possessed the family's last corded phone, an antique now, not quite ancient enough to be rotary but certainly a relic of the days when push-button was still a new thing. A laminated list of frequently-dialed number sat upright on a wire stand that had once been used to display the table number at a relative's wedding. Oscar looked under the line for RICHARD (HOME) and the line for RICHARD (CELL) for the only line he could use tonight, RICHARD (WORK).

He was prepared to hang up in a hurry in the highly unlikely event that a human being was in the office to answer the call at this time of night, but after four rings Richard's recorded message replied, identifying the firm and inviting Oscar to leave a message.

Despite all of his inner rehearsal, Oscar found himself wholly unprepared to speak. "Um."

This was awful, communicating a hesitancy he didn't feel.

"Richard, this is me. Dad. I'm, um, calling a little bit after One AM. I…"

This really was terrible. He hadn't demanded eloquence from himself, but he had promised to deliver a sharp blow, instead of a parade of false taps.

"I'm sorry to leave this message on your office phone, but I didn't want to wake you with it. I'd rather you just get it when you make it into the office, in the morning."

He swallowed.

"I always felt terrible that I wasn't a better father to you and your sister. I did my best. I know it wasn't enough. You're better at it than I was. But I tried. I love you. I…"

Now his voice had almost broken, the image of Deanna's ruined face was rising in him like a cancer, and he found himself in serious danger of bequeathing his only son a message that spent too much time filling him with useless dread.

"I just killed your mother."

There. The rest would be easier, now.

"She didn't suffer. It was very quick. I made sure of that. I did it with love, whatever that means. I did it because I didn't think there was anything left for us. In a few minutes I'm going to join her. It's for the best."

He almost hung up.

"I know you're going to be very angry with me but I want you to do what I say this one last time. You need to call the police and meet them at the house, but please, whatever you do, don't go inside yourself, not until we've been taken away. Your mother or I would never want you to see us like this. Please follow my wishes on that."

A last thought occurred to him. "If you see your sister again, don't let her think it was her fault. This has nothing to do with her. I'm serious. It has nothing to do with her, or with you. It was just that…the time had come. That's all."

He hesitated one last time, putting off the inevitable, aware that the two words to follow would be the last two words there would ever be.

Then he said, "Goodbye, son."

He hung up the phone, surprised that his overwhelming emotion now was not sadness, but relief. The most difficult part was done, with perhaps a few too many missteps and false starts, but with a level of rational calm that would help Richard hold on to his own in the difficult hours ahead.

The parade of lasts continued. That had been his last phone call and his last message to his son. There were any number of other last things he could do now, like perhaps straighten up a bit before pulling the trigger on himself, but for all he knew his son's office had night-time cleaning staff, not some recent immigrant legal or otherwise who couldn't understand enough English to comprehend the meaning of the alien words coming from the speaker, but someone with a command of the language who could take immediate steps to make sure the police got involved now and not hours from now. He had a deadline now. He needed to do whatever else needed to be done quickly.

He brought his glass to the sink (his last time doing that), and left the kitchen (his last time doing that), stopping at the thermostat to do the police a favor by turning the air conditioning up as high as it could possibly go (his last time, ever, fiddling with that little dial).

Returning to the bedroom, he walked right past the terrible carnage on the bed and into the master bathroom, where for the very last time in his life he stopped to pee, sparing his imminent corpse the least of its upcoming releases.

He flushed, put the seat down, and lowered the cover on top of it, aware that this was the last time he would perform any of these simple acts.

Out of custom, he washed his hands again, and forever.

He turned off the bathroom lights and got into bed beside his wife, discovering as he did that he had counted his remaining steps after all. Thirty-seven. That might not have been enough to get out to the mailbox and back. But he had taken the last of those while alive, and now he pulled the blanket up over himself for the last time.

He opened his bedside drawer and removed his revolver.

It was all too easy to keep fueling his obsession over the paucity of time he had left. What was it now? Certainly less time than it would take to listen to even the longest favorite song, possibly less time than it took to sit through the average commercial on television. How many breaths still remained? Ten? Five?

He could lose himself in counting, slicing the time in smaller and smaller increments until even the seconds had no more meaning than the last few years.

The only remaining decision for Oscar, as he clamped his teeth around the barrel, was whether to fire at the roof of his mouth or at the back of his throat. He had read arguments in favor of both methods, differing on which one was less likely to leave him a hopeless vegetable or, worse, an intact mind trapped by misadventure in a body that couldn't see or hear or move. The consensus, he'd found, was that neither method offered absolute certainty of success. Freak trajectories happen. Sometimes people survived as warm meat, befouling their sheets years after a just God would have had them achieve ambient room temperature. From what Oscar understood, a controlled trajectory toward the back of the mouth offered the closest possible thing to a guarantee, though if he beat the odds and became something that had to be wired up to machines, he sure had no idea who he could see to invoke that guarantee for refund.

Doing the job while lying down made the shot he wanted more difficult than he'd expected, so he pulled himself up and scooted up against the headboard, using it as backrest.

The barrel was colder in his mouth than he'd imagined.

How much time left now? Twenty seconds? Ten?

He considered delaying long enough to say something pithy to Deanna, something that would communicate to the air if not to her spirit that he'd done what he'd done in full memory of how much he'd once loved her.

No.

His only remaining question was whether he would hear the shot.

As it happened, he did not.

He had the fleeting sensation of noise and light, but not enough time for his brain to analyze it and identify the only thing it could signify.

He was not aware of his bowels letting go, his heart stopping, the arm that held the revolver falling to one side and landing beside him, as if what he held was not a weapon but a novel that had put him to sleep. Guilt, memory, wonder, thought, sensation, and morality all became parts of his past. Right or wrong, it was over.

The haze swirled. All was darkness.

Then Deanna's corpse, speaking in a voice wet and polluted by fragments of itself, asked him, "Did you lock the front door?"

Oscar's corpse pursed its lips, bloodying them further, answering with the aggrieved reluctance of a thing that would rather remain asleep. "Yes."

"Can you check?"

His corpse sighed. "Yes."

It lifted a flap of blanket and trudged from the room, leaving shiny pieces of itself behind. It was not capable of emotion or conscious thought, and indulged in none on the way, but any witness observing its demeanor as it made its way to the front of the house and tested the knob would have found the implied attitude easy to read: a sense of the formalities being observed, and of the rituals being respected.

The errand took less than a minute.

Then what was left of the man followed its greasy trail back to bed, pulled the covers up over itself, and moved no more.

BIG STUPE AND THE BURIED BIG GLOWING BOOGER

Between scratching his ass and killing folks, Big Stupe still dreams about the golden city sometimes. He didn't spend much of his life there, just a little bit when he was just a baby, but from his crib he was able to look to the window and see towers that touched the scarlet sky, and little flying things zipping back and forth between them, like blue flies excited about a turd. It was something to keep him entertained when he wasn't doing baby things like gurgling and making folk art of his diapers.

Now, all these years later, he's in a place that doesn't have a red sky but a blue one and his adoptive family won't even let him out of the cellar anymore, because it's so tough to corral him whenever he's not around the buried big glowing booger.

The last straw was what he did about five years ago when the youngest, the late Junior Teeth, hit him in the face with a shovel. The gesture didn't hurt Big Stupe any, doing more damage to the shovel, but Big Stupe was so irritated by the insult that he hooked two fingers into Junior Teeth's nostrils and flung him about a mile over the tree line. Poor Junior Teeth landed face-first on a stump, acquired the facial geography of a frying pan, and went simple, not that he ever had two thoughts to rub together in the first place. For the six months he lived after that he wasn't much good for anything except as a dispenser of moans and farts.

Paw ordered Big Stupe into the cellar while the boy he'd been was still all broken up about what he'd done. Little Stupe, as we was called then, had thought this was just like all the other disagreeable occasions when he was shut up with the buried big glowing booger, and had gone without argument, figuring that he'd be let out sooner or later. But the cellar is where he's stayed, filthy and miserable and bored with nothing to do but kill anyone the family tossed in, pretty much all the five years since then. When Big Stupe thinks about it he just figures he shouldn't have made such a bother about that smack from the shovel.

What keeps Big Stupe in the cellar is the buried big glowing booger. Even as a little one Big Stupe's always been sick and out-of-sorts whenever around it, which is even now enough to take most of what makes him Big Stupe away, leaving him a drawn, dry-heaving invalid even if he is still strong as a hundred men. He's too uninspired to even consider escape no matter how many times big brother Razorface comes down to hit him with the booger stick. The booger stick hurts. It's just a pool cue, but Paw's attached a pebble-sized piece of the booger to the tip and it can cut through Big Stupe's skin like nothing else can. A few whacks from that thing, and any thought of fight just drains out of him, like piss from a bucket.

It could be worse. It took a lot of trial and error that sometimes meant bringing Big Stupe to the brink of death for Paw to figure out how deep they had to bury the booger to keep him from causing trouble but also refrain from killing him outright. They don't want him dead, because he's too useful. But without the booger, he's as much a danger to the family as he is to anyone they feed him. With the booger, he's kind of like he's their one-eyed junkyard dog they chain up and beat just enough to remind him it's his job to be mean.

Even so, life in the cellar is not quite as bad as the family – which with Junior Teeth gone means drooling old Grampaw, mean old Maw and Paw, simple-minded cousin Pighead, and downright unpleasant big brother Razorface -- reckon. The darkness doesn't even bother Big Stupe anymore; a couple of years back, brand new developments started happening to his one remaining eye, and he can pretty much see anything he wants now. Even in the pitch of the cellar it's it like he's standing in the middle of the yard at high noon. He can see things even if they're really small, like bugs and germs and whatnot, and the doings of the cellar's worms, in their labyrinths of dirt, can occupy him for hours. Even walls and ceilings don't block his sight these days, since he can see through most things, and distance isn't one bit of a problem either, and he's whacked an awful lot of eetee pud to pretty girls obliviously taking showers in cities fifty or hundred or even thousands of miles away, all over the world, really. He might as well have five hundred channels.

But most of what he watches is the fun the family gets up in between feeding him.

So he shuffles about and watches that old emaciated mummy Grampaw, drooling in his kennel in the corner; straggly-white haired Paw, with the one yellow tooth sticking down like a corn kernel; bingo-armed and pinheaded Maw, with her high-pitched giggle and receding forehead; big brother Razorface, who's called that because he's given himself a mouth full of nails and screws and decorated his nose, cheeks and forehead with blades that could right skin a potato; and cousin Pighead, who would be called that even without his upturned nose because of the generations of inbreeding that gave him a cute little corkscrew tail at the base of his spine, that obliges him to cut a hole in the appropriate part of his the faded blue overalls.

Today they've having family fun time with the half dozen passengers of a van they pulled off the highway, most of them dead and hanging on the pantry meat hooks already, the only survivors as of now a skinny city boy with buck teeth and a pretty girl with hair like spun gold and one thumb-sized beauty mark at the base of her chin.

Razorface's been beating on the city boy just to get him used to the idea that the good part of his life is over and whatever short time is left is going to be one big stinking heap of worse. The blonde girl's gone simple from fear, which is funny since there's not all that much that's been done to her yet; mostly, Paw's just been yanking her about by the hair while Razorface and Pighead made her watch as her friends got cut up with hedge-trimmers.

The city boy's still got some sass in him, though. A little while back he even broke Razorface's nose. But then Maw tripped him up with her cane and he went down with the side of his head against the edge of the coffee table, knocking him half silly, and they were able to descend on him in a pack, each of them taking a little piece of him just to make the point that this was objectionable in their eyes.

Down in the cellar Big Stupe lurches about, making the guttural noises that are all he's been able to make since he was a baby and things like his tongue were still soft enough to get cut out. His grunts become moans and the moans become howls. He keeps it down, though. He can howl loud enough to be heard in town if he wants, and not just here on the twenty acres of Maw and Paw's spread so many miles into the back-country. He knows this because the last time he went all out, he narrowed his one good eye to focus past the walls of the cellar past the dirt past the trees past every obstruction between here and the one broad street of mostly empty storefronts that constitutes Hadleyburg and the nearest thing this part of the state has to civilization, and he saw all the folks in town all stop whatever they're doing and wonder about that distant inhuman sound that keeps disturbing their peace. But then Paw tossed in some extra pieces of the glowing booger he kept around for emergencies and Big Stupe got so sick he almost shit himself blind. He came so close to death that after a couple of days Razorface came down and cleaned up the extra bits so he could recover a mite.

But there is a certain volume at which Big Stupe is allowed to howl, which is only about as loud as that friendly golden retriever that once wandered onto the property and that now hangs, inexpertly stuffed, over the fireplace along the sizable family collection of flattened roadkill taxidermy. His howl penetrates up through the murk and past the ceiling that is the rest of the family's floor and sets the blonde girl broken in the corner to screaming *what the hell is that* the way so many of them do.

Maw tells the city boy that it's time he met the rest of the family, and lets Pighead and Razorface hold on to him while she and Paw pull up the mat of mismatched skin shades they use as a living room rug, and pull up the creaking trap door. Even after everything they've done to him the boy almost manages to fight his way loose, but the family holds on, and the as the dim light of the fly-infested living room streams down into the greater darkness which is Big Stupe's home, they drag the kid and the girl over to the hole and force them to look.

Big Stupe expects their gape-jawed reaction, because he's as ugly as ugly can be. These days, a body could rest the twin barrels of a sawed-off shotgun against his head before pulling the trigger and accomplish nothing but blowing apart a perfectly good gun, but a long time ago he used to bleed and scar up like a normal person, or at least as much like a normal person as this family's got. The handsome face he started with might have grown up to have now resembles nothing as much as a one-eyed rotten hamburger, and always will. It always gets a reaction right away, which is the whole point, even if that's not all of what's so scary about Big Stupe, who Paw cools genuine proof that the Jew government's always been lying to ordinary people about the existence of eetees.

Pighead gives the city boy one last shove, and down he falls, face-planting in the dirt littered with bone fragments and Big Stupe's old dried eetee turds. He doesn't break his neck and ruin the fun the way so many of them do, but instead lurches to his feet in as much of a hurry as he can manage, his hands curled into a pair of ridiculous city fists as Big Stupe steps into the light.

Big Stupe doesn't have to be Big Stupe for the kid to look screwed. The city boy's slight and soft, and has flabby pencil arms, with one eye already half-closed from the whupping Pighead and Razorface gave him. Big Stupe's got a good seven inches of height advantage, even if all these years of living in the cellar have put him in the habit of slouching; also a massive chest and bulging arms and an abdomen that looks capable of taking a battering ram – and has in fact taken a lot worse than that, because Razorface tried one of his hedge-trimmers a couple of years back and all that accomplished was grind the teeth to flat nubs.

What might give the city boy hope is that Big Stupe's got lots of scars too, all across his chest and what's left of his face, only the upper right-hand corner left untouched by the various whuppings Maw and Paw gave him in his early years. This would seem to testify that he can be hurt, but what the city boy doesn't know is that these marks are all at least eight years old and it's been a bit since Maw and Paw have been able to discipline him properly. What the scars do, really, is just fool folks into thinking they've got a chance, when they would have better odds taking on a battleship in a slap-fight.

Up above, the family cackles at the edges of the trap door, and the girl screams; but down here, that's just background noise, as Big Stupe takes a slow, shuffling step forward, like one of those gauze-wrapped geeks from the old mummy movies.

The city boy snatches up a discarded human femur and charges, bringing it down against the lattice of scars on Big Stupe's forehead. It powders on impact. The city boy falls back, then elects to go for Big Stupe's eyes and rushes forward again, this time with thumbs foremost, his left clawing at the ragged hole on the right side of Big Stupe's face, and his right clawing at the one bright blue eye that the family's let Big Stupe keep.

For a moment the city boy looks like he thinks he's winning. Then he frowns, registering disorientation, disbelief, and finally astonishment. Big Stupe doesn't need education to read what he's thinking. The surface his thumb has found is definitely an eye. It has the curve of an eye and even the wet veneer of an eye, but it's not giving ground to the thumb. *What is it?* the boy must think. *A glass eye? Is this big geek blind?* Then he figures out that what he's touching is an eye too tough to pop. Trying to gouge this eye is like trying to scratch his initials in marble. It's a monument.

And that's before it turns hot as a welder's torch.

The city boy staggers back. That thumb is smoking and sparking like a marshmallow that's fallen into a campfire. The melted flesh dribbles down the sides of the hand like melted candle-wax, and as he falls to his knees, insane with agony, another flash of heat slices the cellar in a cruel arc. The arm that ends in that ruined hand just separates from the city boy's shoulder, both severed and cauterized.

The city boy shrieks again.

Up above, the blonde girl makes sounds like she's finally figured out that screams do no Earthly good and she needs to invent something else on another auditory spectrum that might prove more helpful. Razorface hoots like he's getting his wing-wang serviced. Pighead gibbers like a monkey. Maw and Paw holler at Big Stupe to finish it. Always willing to please, Big Stupe tilts his asymmetrical head, figuring out which of several different methods he should use to do the job, and finally strides forward to cup the kid's forehead in his hand.

Then he closes his fist, reducing everything he's just grasped to soggy powder.

• • • •

Big Stupe is never hungry. He hasn't needed food, the way normal folks do, since he was still permitted the outside and daylight started starting feeding him more in terms of nutrition than any scraps of meat he could forage or the few scraps the family deigned to toss him.

Daylight's so good for him that it keeps him strong even when he's in the shade, or underground. These days he can stand stock still in the center of his cellar and feel that nourishing sun stream through the roof, through the attic with its collection of license plates, through the human taxidermy studio Maw and Paw have made of the second floor, through the living room where most of the family fun takes place, and through the floor, all the way to where he stands in the cellar dirt, and feels as sated as jowly restaurant patron letting out his belt a notch or two. Of late it's made being so close to the buried big glowing booger almost tolerable.

No, it's not a question of hunger. But Big Stupe still likes eating *food* food from time to time, and so he spends the hour or so after Maw and Paw shut him in and plunge him back into what most people consider darkness eating the kind of meal he's always been taught to appreciate. He especially enjoys the brains. With the front of his latest kill's head peeled off, the skull functions as a fine-cook pot, and the grey matter is a ready-to-eat meal, sizzling in its own juices the instant Big Stupe gives it some of the burning heat from his eye.

Big Stupe gets down on his hands and knees and laps at this soup like a dog. Then, bored, he spends a few minutes whacking his pud, drilling another impact bore-hole in cinderblock already as full of impact points as a honeycomb. Then he crawls off to the corner farthest from the center of the room, where the buried big glowing booger doesn't irritate him as much as it does elsewhere. It is also the site of an ancient coal pile and, aside from murder and whacking off, the only real source of amusement the family's left him. He sits there for a spell, squeezing the black lumps until they become glittery white ones, before drifting off and descending into the dreams that make him happy for a while.

He doesn't dream about the golden city this time. He dreams about a long time spent in the cramped tube that followed, tended by mechanical arms while looking out a glass pane into an infinite darkness where the stars raced by like streaks of light. He dreams about all that ending with great heat and a sudden impact, his glass cracking and after that his first introduction to the crawling agony of the big glowing booger, which hit the ground just a few feet from where his rocket has. He dreams about the relief of being carried out of the booger's range by a man with white hair and compassionate smile, who brings him over to a woman whose own face is just as generous, just as marked by smile-lines. He dreams about being that baby, held by those people, confused by the lines on their faces, when he's really looking for the young and noble-looking couple in the brightly light room with the golden city outside the window. He dreams about how bothersome it was, looking for that city and finding only an endless expanse of dirt, dotted here and there with what little patches of green. He dreams that this makes making no sense to him.

The most comprehensible moment in the dream comes when the kindly couple climb out of the blackened trench his cradle made when it skipped along the earth, only to find Paw's pickup truck parked behind their own, and Paw getting out, looking deceptively friendly.

On that the dream draws a clotted red curtain.

He then gets a taste of another dream that afflicts him from time to time, that's even worse, because it's a good one, and with the life he's lived he's got no excuse for such a thing. In it, there's city a lot like that one with the glittering golden spires except different, that he somehow soars above as an inhabitant of the bright blue sky that Maw and Paw deny him. In the dream he is aware that he is the city's god, or not its god but something else that is not in his vocabulary, in any event the presence that the people of the city gaze up at and adore. None of this makes any sense to him, but it does make him sad, and as frequently happens he wakes weeping from his one good eye, knowing only that something fine has been taken from him, and put in a place where he will never ever be able to find it.

Of course, he also wakes knowing that he is now longer alone, because big brother Razorface is now in the cellar with him. This is not good news. Razorface isn't like Big Stupe; he's human, more or less, though Maw and Paw have changed him in some ways, and all of those ugly and mean. But he hates Big Stupe with a passion, and he for the last few years Maw and Paw have let him function as Big Stupe's primary disciplinarian. He kicks Big Stupe in the ribs, an act that wouldn't hurt at all if there weren't some of the big glowing booger sewn into his boot linings. He also jabs Big Stupe with the booger stick, drawing welts. He doesn't have a tongue any more than Big Stupe does, but unlike Big Stupe he has no problem with speaking in his distorted way, and as he hurls abuse down at his despised eetee brother he speaks words that Big Stupe has no trouble cleaning up and filtering into coherent meaning. *Get your ass up, you lazy shit! I brung you something!*

Big Stupe could liquefy Razorface with a glance, but chooses not to. Instead he just makes his mouth a grim straight line and lets Razorface imagine that happening. Razorface backs off, still holding the tip of the booger stick before him. Behind him, in the darkness, past the shaft of dusty light and the carpenter's ladder that Razorface uses on his rare descents into his dangerous little brother's prison , the sole survivor of the last car of visitors, the girl, sits curled up as closely pressed to the far wall as possible. She is not as hysterical as she was before, but she shows the signs of a long day spent with no one but the family for company, mostly big black marks on her bare arms and the swollen welts on her jaw. Surprisingly, nothing's been removed from her, not so much as a finger. She's even been changed into an old-fashioned blouse that used to belong to Grammaw, with a pattern of yellowing daisies on it.

Razorface leers with the row of screws and carpenter's nails he's imbedded in his upper gums. *That's right, you big freak! You get her! I wanted Maw and Paw to give her to me but they're givin' her to you!*

Big Stupe doesn't understand why this particular bequest makes Razorface so angry, since the blonde girl wouldn't be the first ever tossed in his cellar at the end of a fun session upstairs, but his momentary look of confusion only earns another savage prod with the stick.

As your wife, you stupid ape!

Oh, well now. That's quite different.

Big Stupe is aware of the concept of sex for fun and for procreation, and has sometimes whiled away the hours watching people rut in various combinations in distant cities all over the world, but has never quite imagined that he might ever get to have any himself, a prospect that will of course require him to exercise some careful control over his issue's escape velocity. In truth, he's not entirely sure that the trick can be done. He's never given it any thought before.

He understands why Razorface is so riled up, though. Fornication has never been a common thing in this house, not since Grammaw was still around and shaking the roof with her cries of pleasure at her regular rooting by her brother, Grampaw. Maw and Paw, their twin children, have been known to do it on a boring night or two, but their tastes don't run to that sort of thing so much as making sport of whatever city folk they manage to run off the road. But sex remains one of Razorface's more powerful drives, even if Maw and Paw have never given him permission to indulge it with people and have thus far only permitted him to practice on pigs. The news that his younger brother, the eetee, is going to have some long before he ever gets to must come as a bitter life disappointment.

Big Stupe can only grunt a wordless apology that it isn't his idea.

This only earns him another savage kick in the ribs. *It ain't about fun, you geek! It's about making more eetee babies for the family!*

The very point of the buried big glowing booger is that it sickens and weakens him, and in fact reduces him to a state that, while very powerful by the standards of most other people, is still his equivalent of walking around with a hundred-plus fever, and pneumonia, and a stomach flu. He pukes out half his kill as it is, and the kick in the belly, in concert with resentment over Razorface's treatment of him, makes this hurl one well beyond those known to mortal men. Razorface is flung halfway across the basement from the force of the impact, before he even hits dirt again, and when he gets up he is even more irate than before, because in his case biting his lower lip during a sudden jolt means piercing it in a half a dozen places. His jaw runs slick with blood. He looks like he would like to kick Big Stupe again, but he thinks better of it. He climbs back up the living room, pulling the ladder up after himself before shutting the trap door, and plunging Big Stupe and the girl in darkness.

Now, this is an entirely new situation for Big Stupe, who has had visitors he was supposed to rip to pieces before, but never one he was supposed to make babies with.

He knows the basic procedure, from his distant observations of honeymoon couples in faraway places. What he hasn't figured out is the etiquette, a concept he's aware of but hasn't had to practice all that much in his everyday life. It does matter to him. Though he's eviscerated and eaten any number of people, he's always tried to be a good person, even if the family's definition of good isn't what most people would approve of. He can't just force her. This is his wife he's talking about.

So he rises from his end of the cellar, shuffles past the dirt mound that causes him the worst of his burning discomfort, and makes his way to the girl, who sobs and blubbers and presses himself closer to her cinderblock wall, at his approach. He looks at her the way he looks at no other stranger who's ever shared this cellar with him, as a person who it's now his duty to get to know, and it occurs to him not just that she'd be right pretty if she was cleaned up a little, but that she has the hazel eyes of an angel and behind them a soul that he can imagine resonating with his own. He touches her pretty cheek and she releases an ear-piercing shriek, which is not uncommon among folks who wind up in the darkness with him, but is downright disturbing from a girl who's supposed to be his bride. He has however seen weddings from a distance, the way he sees everything, and he knows that it's not unheard of for brides to weep with happiness. So maybe that's what she's doing now. He grunts and touches her cheek again. She shrieks more loudly, and he withdraws to his coal pile, thinking that it's good to be married but that maybe it's the sort of thing that both he and his bride need to get used to.

For a time he contents himself with watching her as she clings to the wall, weeping and carrying on almost as if she's still a kill and not some brand new member of the family.

After a while, he shifts randomly and she cries, "I can hear you, you bastard," which makes him curse himself for being such an idiot. Of course she needs to *hear* him; she doesn't have eetee eyes like his and can't *see* him. He needs to furnish their honeymoon palace with at least enough light for her to get around, so she's comfortable. He plunges his arm through the cinderblocks behind him, roots around a mite, and pulls out a tree root the diameter of his own bicep, then delivers it to where she cowers. A few seconds later it is aflame, and a glow rises, making shadows dance all over the cellar.

His bride hollers again, never more shrilly than when she sees him stooped over her, head tilted, gazing down at her in search of approval. This makes him retreat again.

He remains on his coal pile, brooding, for the several minutes it takes her to stir from her chosen spot beside the wall to one slightly closer to the glowing embers, and warm her hands.

The air gets hazy, and she starts to cough.

Then the trap door swings open, the ladder descends, and Razorface comes down, looking pissed off, though it must be said of him that he never looks jolly. He's as mean as a donkey kicking itself in the ass. His chin is still bloody, because he somehow hasn't gotten around to unstapling his lower lip yet, and his overalls still bears the spatter of high-velocity eetee hurl. The girl goes back against the wall to escape him, but he's not after her, not this time. He stamps the fire out and whips out his wang to piss on the smoking embers, an act that doesn't make the girl any happier. He yells something even more incoherent than usual because of the stapled lips, something that translates to, *Don't start no fires!*, and heads back upstairs. This time they pull up the ladder but don't shut the trap door, because they're resigned to the idea that Big Stupe's kind of slow on the uptake and that this project might require more in the way of active animal husbandry. Paw yells, *get a move on, already, you eetee fuckwit!*

Big Stupe doesn't much like being pressured on this his wedding night. But their yelling has given him an idea. Since it's her attitude that needs adjustment, it's her attitude he's going to work on. This time, when he shuffles toward the girl, he takes something from his coal pile with him. He doesn't back away from her screams; he just takes her by the wrist, pulls it toward him, and places a glittering object about the size of an egg in her unwilling palm.

She's terrified, but eager to appease him. "I d-don't understand. This looks like a dia--"

Of course, he would say if he had the time and the ability, *you're my wife, this is what I'm supposed to give you, this is what is supposed to make you like me, so we can get on with making babies.* She would no doubt perceive these words as incoherent grunts and moans, at least at first, at least until she got used to minding him, but he is prepared to sincerely win her heart.

But big brother Razorface has never shown that kind of patience, and so he shouts something angry about how that does beat all and lowers the ladder so he can come back down and start whacking at Big Stupe with the booger stick. The glowing tip raises a painful welt every time it hits the bunched muscles of Big Stupe's back, but for six hits or so Big Stupe pays it no mind, because he's too busy meeting the girl's pair of frightened hazel eyes with his single blue one, and letting her know that what he intends to be sincere in his promises.

Then Razorface says, *fine, I'll take her for myself then*, and reaches past him to grab her by the hair.

This turns out to be Big Stupe's last straw.

He stands up, straighter than he's ever stood up before, and back-hands Razorface into the dirt.

Razorface lands twice before rolling the last bit, up against the edge of the ladder, wheezing and moaning because that's what you do when a couple of your ribs turn to gravel. He tries to grab for the booger stick, but it's gone flying somewhere and isn't convenient anymore. He glances over his shoulder at Big Stupe, who's standing straight and tall with his one good eye glowing red, and realizes that escape is the better part of valor. But his own first attempt to stand fails him. He grabs at the highest rung he can and pulls himself to his knees.

Behind Big Stupe, the girl suddenly seems to understand that he's somehow become an ally. *"Don't let him get away! He'll pull up the ladder!"*

Well, at least she's talking to him, now. And or Big Stupe, who is constitutionally inclined to respect the rules as he understands them, to stand for Maw, Paw, and the family way, what she just said is a literally revolutionary idea. He tilts his head, seriously considering it. Chief among his considerations is the understanding that though he doesn't need a well-lit place to see his new bride clearly, she does have the kind of hair that would glow in sunlight, and that this would be a sight to see. Besides, he's frankly tired of his family's shit.

Razorface, who sees him considering this, hauls himself to a standing position. Up above, Maw and Paw and Pighead screech at him, telling him to hurry his fool ass if he don't want to get locked in the basement with Big Stupe. Maw, showing a degree of maternal concern that has never come out of her even once in all these years, even stretches out one bony crone arm to pull Razorface up. But than a sudden rising heat makes the flesh on her wrist bubble and turn black, and she pulls that arm back, shrieking.

Big Stupe drills his fingers into Razorface's shoulders. The grip penetrates skin, muscle and bone, all in one go, the fingers as hard as railroad spikes that stop only when they've descended to knuckle-depth. It makes big brother screech like a sow who's been opened up from neck to tail but hasn't yet bled out enough to figure out it's dead yet. This is a satisfying moment for Big Stupe after all the pokes with the booger stick, but it's still a bit of a miscalculation, since even Big Stupe needs his hands free to climb a ladder and grasping hold of this one will mean first releasing his grip on his big brother, which he's not quite ready to do yet, because there are still things he wants to do to him. Stymied, he peers up at the open square in the ceiling above and thinks forlorn puzzled thoughts about how nice it would be if that bright opening were closer to him than it is.

Then all of a sudden it is, by about a yard.

This surprises him so much he squeaks. He looks down and confirms that his filthy bare feet have left the cellar floor, by about that same distance, and now hang unsupported. Together with Razorface's they almost resemble the legs of a Jesus carving that's been pried loose of its crucifix, if that Jesus figure were also carrying a hated brother by bloody finger-holes driven into his shoulders, whose clothed legs were kicking and thrashing alongside the carving's serene and naked ones.

This interests Big Stupe.

It also refreshes him. It's amazing how much difference three more feet make. There is now that much more distance between him and the buried big glowing booger, which still hurts but doesn't weaken him quite as much as it did when he was standing at dirt level. At the same time the nourishing rays of the sun feel even more present, two ceilings and a shingle roof above him, and it occurs to him that if he wants to feel better he really needs to do more of this flying thing, and faster. And so he turns his single eye upward, at the opening that has now lurches closer by about an inch or so.

The blade of a hoe clangs against the top of his head: Maw, trying to knock him back to the ground. The hoe blade suffers more from the impact than he does. It dents. This doesn't stop Maw from trying again. This time she hilariously misses Big Stupe's head and hits Razorface's instead, cutting a nice slit in his scalp. Big brother twitches, his bowels letting go. But none of her subsequent swings knock Big Stupe back down into the dirt, not with the booger no longer weakening him the way it was, and certainly not with the sun calling to him in the voice of an eager lover spreading her legs and promising that she'll make him feel real fine.

Up, he thinks again, and now the generous sun gives him the gift of speed. He and his fraternal cargo rocket upward, through the ceiling of the living room and through the ceiling of the bedroom shared by Maw and Paw and through the slanted roof and into the open air above, where the sun is as bright and as gold as the hair of Big Stupe's bride and the strength pouring into his back and limbs is not to be believed. This, Big Stupe understands, as he continues his journey into the sky, is the way he's always been meant to feel, every minute of every day, the way his family always kept him from feeling by locking him up with the big glowing booger. It occurs to him, for the first time, from a faraway place suddenly close up, that the way he feels now, all the anger he's felt about that for all these years doesn't have to be an itch he can't scratch.

The kindling his head and broad shoulders have made of three shattered floors of a house tumble from his bare shoulders in clouds of shrapnel and sawdust, but Razorface, who has made the same journey with him, is not as unscathed. His head's now staved in a bunch of additional places other than the wound that Maw inflicted, and there's blood pouring out his ears and long flaps of ragged skin hanging from the places on his arms wherever they turned out to be not quite as good at penetrating wood-frame construction as Big Stupe. He's not quite dead, and might indeed still be capable of surviving the damage done to him if given heroic medical treatment. But even in that unlikely event the face that began the day criss-crossed with scars and studded with nails and screws and loops of barbed wire and the one eye that saw okay but didn't quite line up with the other would never be even *that* presentable again. Razorface has been uglied up considerably, even by his own high standards.

Big Stupe has no problem with this.

He soars upward until Maw and Paw's farmhouse is like a little slate fingernail the altitude renders patches on a quilt, then drops his big brother, just drops him, keeping up with him all the way down just to see if the man's got any awareness of what's happening to him. He doesn't. This is bothersome, but a sideways punch right through the ribcage and out through the spine takes care of the sibling rivalry anyway.

Big Stupe zips through the hole he made in the roof, and doesn't slow down until he's passed through the holes he made in the floors beneath that, and returns to the living room in time to see a fresh ruckus going on at the opening to the cellar. Everybody's screaming, even butt-naked Grampaw in his kennel, though his howls are all excitement, since the years have left him with no more mind than a plucked, liver-spotted old monkey.

The general fuss all seems to have less to do with the damage Big Stupe's done to the house than with the fight taking place at the trap door. Big Stupe's new bride has tried to follow him up the ladder, which shows initiative, but has succeeded in only getting the top of her head above floor level. Maw, doing what she can to make the best of a bad situation, has grabbed her by the long blonde hair and is slapping her back and forth across the cheeks to force her back into the darkness. Both wife and mother scream at Big Stupe to intervene, to *Help! Help!*, and this chorus of cries strikes him as oddly familiar in a way that he can't quite figure out, almost as if it comes from a life he hasn't lived, a life that he might have lived if the family hadn't found him. But he doesn't have the time to remind himself which of the two women he's going to rescue right now, because right there on the other side of the room behind the arm chair with the real human arms is Paw, hands shaking with sudden terrified palsy as he hurries to load his shotgun with some of the emergency rounds he long ago from bits he chipped off the big glowing booger.

Big Stupe dedicates a quick glance to making that shotgun too hot for any human being to hold, so hot that the delicious scent of cooked meat rises and fills the room while Paw screams and drops the weapon, booger ammunition and all.

Pighead, being too dense to do the only sensible thing and run for his life, steps between Big Stupe and the two grappling women like he can talk his adoptive brother out of causing more trouble. Big Stupe, who has had more than enough of him too, makes a move that everybody but him will perceive as no more than a twitch, and Pighead starts yelling his head off, because in that eye-blink his skin's been peeled off him in a single piece and hung from the lighting fixture, unwashed overalls and all, his empty legs stirring in the breeze like freshly laundered long-johns. Pighead himself is red and glistening and just beginning to feel what's been done to him when Big Stupe returns from the kitchen with a fresh canister of Morton's Salt. Liberal application of this sends him to the floor shrieking.

Maw is still slapping Mrs. Stupe and has succeeded in swelling up her lip and eyes some, but Big Stupe yanks her away and hurls her into a corner, beside Grampaw's waist-high kennel, which she collapses against, holding up both her gnarled and calloused hands in a pathetic attempt at self-protection. A respectably-thick lock of blonde hair, six inches long and bloody at the roots, hangs knotted from those fingers. She cries out toothlessly that big Stupe cain't do this to her, that she's his Maw.

By Big Stupe's math, some respect is owed to all these years of maternal devotion and so when he stomps over to where she begs for mercy he takes her face in his hands and forces her trembling chin upward and forces her into a kiss. It's the only kiss their relationship has ever known, and it is not the kind of kiss that normally takes place between mother and adopted son, because it's open-mouthed and would look extremely passionate if his one eye wasn't so cold and her two so terrified.

He's just about ready for the powerful inhale when Paw, who's found the courage to overlook the agony in his hands and try to do something else to stop him, but not the presence of mind to do something that might possibly work, rips the blood-red velvet curtain from the front window and tosses it over both their heads.

This is an attempt at distraction that only makes sense because Big Stupe came by his knack of seeing through objects while living like an animal in the cellar, and Paw hasn't had any opportunity to add that to his mental roster of things the eetee can do. Still, even Paw does seem to realize that this was a dang pointless tactic. Even the various actual implements of death the family's got lying around won't be any more effective, at this point, so he turns tail and aims himself at As Far Away as Possible.

But Paw doesn't even get out of the living room, because the blonde girl brings him to a face-plant with a furious tackle to the knees. He kicks her in the face with one mud-stained boot, rattling her teeth a little, but that's nothing compared to what she's been through already, and so she crawls across his thrashing body like it's an angry sea and she's a determined swimmer, before dipping in close and clamping those teeth on his nose.

Meanwhile, Big Stupe figures that he'd rather not have his head covered any more, thank you, and with a certain angry vibration of his head vaporizes the part of the curtain that covers it. The rest settles down around his shoulders, and that's stupid too, but worth leaving where it is because he's just gotten married and sees it as rank disrespect to the missus to walk around the house naked and covered with dirt. He leaves Maw, who's wide-eyed and not quite dead, but turning blue as the empty red sacs that were her lungs dangle inside-out from her lips. She has time to claw at them as if they're the problem, and she succeeds in making a few desperate tracks in the tissue before her eyes roll back and she topples face-forward onto those sagging little air-bags, which though deflated still manage to pop.

Grampaw hoots like all this is fine comedy. He doesn't have much of a mind anymore and probably doesn't remember everything he ever did to the young Stupe when the boy couldn't do everything he can do now, but Big Stupe can, so he figures he might as well. He kneels, reaches his mighty arm between the bars of the kennel, grabs Grampaw by his withered old neck, and pulls the old bastard's head through the gap between the iron bars. The gap is of course too narrow to allow a head to pass without severe changes in the shape of that head. Big Stupe pulls it out anyway, with a sound like a crunchy wet gunshot. Grampaw needs a second to figure out he's dead. He manages an impressed *wow,* his first recognizable word in seven years, before he slides to the floor, much thinner head and all, brain stuff oozing from the mouth and nostrils and ears.

On the other side of the rubble-strewn living room, past where Pighead writhes on the floor leaving scarlet painting-impressions of himself wherever he rolls, Big Stupe's wife still grapples with Paw. Paw's face looks a lot like a skull now that she's had a chance to gnaw on it for a few seconds and left him without nose or lips to confuse the issue. He still manages to grab her by the wrists and toss her against the human-leg coffee table, before staggering to his feet and deciding once again that getting out of there is still the better part of valor. Leaving a trail of blood from his ravaged face, he barrels out through the mesh of the screen door without bothering to open it. Big Stupe strides across the room in no particular hurry, and while it hurts him a little bit that his blood-drenched but not additionally wounded bride still cries out and cowers when he draws near, he still gently and lovingly guides her to the arm chair with the human arms and eases her down into it, giving her the gentlest of all possible pats on the wrist before he follows Paw out the door.

Outside – and how glorious it is for Big Stupe to feel the direct rays of the sun again – Paw has managed to get to the pickup. It's actually the same pickup he took Big Stupe home in, all those years ago, when he was just a baby and yet to become Big Stupe; the same pickup that hauled home the little dented rocket ship and the big glowing booger. It hasn't been washed once in all the years since, and the original business name painted on the cab has long since been rendered illegible by rust and road dust. Paw's behind the wheel, looking like a raw burger that's just gone ten rounds with a mallet. When he sees Big Stupe emerge from the house, the torn curtain around his shoulders billowing in the dusty wind that's just sprung up, he howls distorted obscenities before he turns the key and heads off into the distance at full acceleration, leaving a trail of dust.

This is no real inconvenience. It actually adds to the enjoyment of it all.

A couple of miles away Paw seems him standing in the road ahead and just naturally tries to run him over, but only succeeds in crumpling the front end of the truck into an insulted V and flinging himself the driver halfway through the ancient windshield. This he surprisingly lives through, even if it as a freshly-minted quadriplegic with shards of glass imbedded in his cheeks and forehead. One eye's got glass in it and is so full of blood it looks like a clown nose, and the other, which can still see, hangs outside its socket by a bloody bundle of nerve fibers. He still tries to curse his son, but can't quite manage the breath.

Big Stupe helpfully inserts Paw's one working eye back into its socket, then assists Paw getting back into the now significantly compressed space behind the wheel, and commences a chassis modification project, at a speed that only he can. He imagines that for Paw it's impossible to follow what's happening except as a blur, accompanying a soundtrack of grinding metal that seems to come from every direction at once. Under Big Stupe's powerful molding fingers the cab constricts around him, conforming itself to the shape of his broken body bit by bit, until it's all so snug that he wouldn't be able to move even if he could, a hermetically sealed coffin with just enough air in it to keep him alive for a while.

This Big Stupe hefts with one hand, even as Paw, entombed in steel, commences screaming at him to stop.

He tosses it up and down in his palm a few times, gauging its weight. To Big Stupe, it's light.

He winds up and tosses it at escape velocity, appreciating the way it glows red as it hits the upper atmosphere, but significantly disappointed when it vaporizes. He'd pictured getting it all the way to outer space. He has never been taught the concept of karma, but he does understand it, and would have liked to go through the rest of his life imagining Paw drifting through the universe, the way he once did himself.

Ah, well. Practice will make perfect.

The sound of distant sobbing and snuffling, back in the direction of home, sends him into the air again. A quick return to the farmhouse and he finds the source: the young Mrs. Stupe, who hasn't stayed put as per his instructions. She's hobbling on bare feet up the dirt road, endearingly trying to make it to the highway before he gets back. She's got a bloody nose, a swollen lip, a bare and bloody patch on her scalp where Maw ripped some of the hair out of her head, bruises up and down her bare arms, skinned knees, and stigmatic feet. She walks as if she's unfamiliar with the concept of merely swinging her arms and instead holds them as if they're creatures as alien to this planet as he is, with her elbows pressed against tight against her ribs and her forearms held out at either side, like steadying wings.

To Big Stupe, she's the loveliest creature in all the world, the first beautiful being he's known in almost as long as he can remember. When he comes to a gentle landing before her, curtain flapping in the breeze, she falters and turns away from him, ready to run.

It turns out that he is in that direction, too.

Another attempt. And another.

She finds him at every compass point, no matter how much she spins.

But neither does he come any closer to her, or make any move to hurt her.

She screams at him, tells him that she saw him kill and eat her boyfriend and that they're not friends, and never will be. She hates him. She wants to get away from him and forget that they ever met. She tells him to die you son of a bitch.

This is a problem.

He zips back to the house, comes back in a heartbeat with two lumps of coal, and makes them into two fresh diamonds, which he cuts to exquisite perfection using his thumbnail. She flings them away, so he zips off and gets some more coal to make new ones. They don't make a dent in her heart either. He keeps doing it, though, and in less than a minute she is standing in the center of a glittering fortune fit for a queen. They threaten to achieve ankle-depth before she finally accepts one from his hand without throwing it away. She weeps, why can't you just let me go? She tells him, it's not his fault, the kind of life his family made him live, the kind of person they made of him. But he needs to understand. Just saying so doesn't make her his wife. That's not right.

He understands. This needs to be consensual. It needs to be based in love. He can also see that she's shivering a little, and not just out of fear, but because the sun has started to go down. So he pulls the curtain from his shoulders and places it on hers, lowering the hole over her head so she can wear it and be warm in the twilight chill.

She says, thank you.

It is the only thing she gets to say, the only thing she'll ever say out loud for the entire rest of her natural life, which will approach the span optimal for women of Earth.

A black dot appears at the center of her forehead.

It is the size of a pinprick, microscopic really, and it testifies to his increased levels of focus. But by shifting the position of his head slightly and directing the heat through that entrance at different angles, he is able to boil off much of what sits in her forebrain, including all of her willfulness, most of her higher intelligence, and any memories capable of luring her anywhere but to his side.

He has learned a great deal, looking through things like heads, about the ways the meat inside them works...and he's learning even more, by doing.

Soon, he thinks, while still working on the project, he'll fix up the house real nice, replace all the old human-part furniture with brand new décor of the same sort but better preserved, and start taking his own trips to the highway and more distant locations, to collect folks for the nightly family entertainment -- and not just the pathetic handful at a time that Maw and Paw and Pighead and Razorface ever managed, because at the speed he works he figures he and the missus can enjoy themselves some nights in the upper three digits, plucked out of distant places like St. Louis and Paris and Bangkok and Islamabad and Melbourne. The cellar and the big glowing booger he'll keep, even if he never heads down there himself, just in case the kids breed true. There's always a need for discipline, when children get unruly.

The modifications to Mrs. Stupe take less than a minute. After a few seconds of shuddering with wisps of black smoke emerging from the black mark on her forehead, a black mark that will never go away but will soon heal up and look like a cute freckle, she opens her eyes. Dazed and uncomprehending and not distracted by nearly as much brain as she had before, she shows only a moment of distress before her eyes, no longer lining up quite as well as they did, focus on the face of the figure standing before her. For her, deprived of everything else, it must be like being born, and first seeing the face of the being meant to love her.

He smiles at her.

Grateful for a guiding cue, she smiles back.

Then the man from the stars takes her hand and leads her back to the family home, where they, but not many others, are fated to live happily after ever.

ROTTEN LITTLE TOWN:
AN ORAL HISTORY (ABRIDGED)

It's been over twenty years since the last episode of Rotten Little Town, the smash hit occult western that ran for six seasons between 1993 and 1999, plus one two-hour reunion movie released in 2000 that wrapped up most of the dangling storylines in such dramatic fashion that it remains highly debated today. Completing its planned arc despite the untimely deaths of one creator and two lead actors, plus multiple other mishaps, the show is still fondly remembered as the compelling story of Sheriff Horace T. Booker and his efforts to clean up the frontier town of Sawblade, New Mexico, which is beset by supernatural forces, at the height of the wild west. The creators and surviving cast members agreed to talk to us about how the show came to be, the rigors of filming, the show's popularity and legacy, and the chances of a return to the town where, as the theme song put it, "Darkness had a name."

The Early Days
JERRY STRACKER (Co-Creator): You must understand that in those days most episodic television did not have "arcs." It had self-contained stories, that always returned the characters to status quo at the end of each hour-long episode. You could have series lasting seven, eight or nine years and nothing would change at all, unless there were kids who grew up on camera. I always wanted to do something more substantial, something that functioned as a novel for television. And I was still

musing about how to do that when I mentioned it to [co-creator] Barth Lawrence, who told me that he'd been working on some ideas along that line, for a western series he then called *Booker*. He showed me what he had, and I fell on it with both hands, ripped it apart and put it back together before getting a pilot deal.

How much of his original vision made it to air?

JERRY STRACKER: Less than you'd think. Barth pretty much wanted to do a standard TV western about a troubled lawman holding his town together by sheer force of will, and of course, plenty of bullets. He just didn't know how to sell any of the networks a western in that day and age. I mean, that was the era of *Dances With Wolves* and *Unforgiven*, but the genre was still considered pretty much dead, and though it was his dream project, he had no idea how to make it work. I was the one who said, but what if we add the supernatural? What if we took Booker's arch enemy, the bad man Hogarth Malloy, and put him in league with the actual devil? Do that, I said, and we can give you six years' worth of episodes, a story that built from year to year. He was ecstatic.

He was said to hate horror fiction.

JERRY STRACKER: Yes, he was resistant at first, but then I showed him how adding this one fantasy element could turn the whole show into a great morality play. Honestly, he came around to loving it.

We have a letter showing that he tried to get you fired off the development team, ten days before the car accident.

JERRY STRACKER: Barth was like that. He would try to fire you one minute, then be your brother five minutes later. It made him difficult to work with. The backers called us in and he talked about the purity of his original vision and I talked about how I had made it better, and they said that if I was dropped from the project they would have to drop him, too. Honestly, it was that obvious. But after we left the room, we had a great dinner and came to terms. We were, he admitted, making two shows in one, a western and a supernatural thriller, and if he stuck to his wheelhouse and made sure everything was authentic on the western end, he could do a bunch of episodes every year where the arc was in the background, and his more realistic take was more prominent; I would do the balance, the supernatural end, and I think he saw that I just wanted what was best for the show.

How did you take it when he died?

JERRY STRACKER: Well, first, of course, he disappeared, and that was worrisome, because he was so unstable, and we were all afraid that he'd done something foolish. He'd had his problems with drugs, you know. When the car was found, upside-down in that ditch, we were all stunned and heartbroken. He was a genius, even if he did have a vision for the show that was not quite in line with my own. Do you know that he drowned in six inches of water? Horrifying. I think about him every day.

Didn't he scratch the word "Murder" on the upholstery?

JERRY STRACKER: That came many years later from an investigator trying to sell a book, and I don't believe a word of it.

It's a sensitive question, but how much of his original vision remained in the show bible?

JERRY STRACKER: Almost none. Our protagonist kept his name, but otherwise became a completely different person. The town changed, the tone changed, the arc changed, almost all of his characters were thrown out and replaced with my own—honestly, his spirit is all over the show, I think, and we were sufficiently sentimental about him to put a couple of his stories in season one, but otherwise, it's largely the work of me and other writers in the stable. It's a very different show than he wanted, at the onset, but I think he would have approved. I insist on it.

The Pilot Movie

Following the death of its original creator, Rotten Little Town went to pilot, using a script credited to both Stracker and Lawrence. It was the only time Sheriff Horace T. Booker was played by an actor other than Elliot James, who would go on to achieve stardom in the part. We reached out to original Booker, Cliff Adams, at the Actors Retirement Home in Los Angeles.

CLIFF ADAMS (original actor, "Sheriff Horace T. Booker"): It was such a long time ago that I don't remember the story at all. I didn't think it was any better or worse than anything else I'd worked on at the time, and I sure as hell didn't expect it to go to series.

JERRY STRACKER: Cliff was everything we were hoping for at the time: an older, iconic actor known for westerns, all attributes that were pretty thin on the ground in those days. Bruce Dern had said no, and so had Sam Elliott, and we just kind of fell on Adams, who embodied the milieu even if he'd always been a supporting player. At the time we thought we'd struck gold.

CLIFF ADAMS: How long did that thing last, ten years? Eight? Crap, I would have hated that. TV hours were already a bit rough on me at that age. I wasn't exactly a workaholic.

JERRY STRACKER: Let's just say that he needed excessive hand-holding.

ARLENE MOLINEAUX (actor, "Kitty Parsons"): The man was a legend—or so I thought, from the perspective of a twenty-three-year-old actress who'd just been handed her first big break—but he wasn't . . . (*pause*) He didn't exactly understand the premise. He kept saying that the show would be a lot better if we just got rid of all the supernatural hugger-mugger. He used that phrase. "Hugger-mugger."

BUDDY SAMS (actor, "Toby Samson"): That's right! "Hugger-mugger!" In four days, I was already sick as shit of him saying that! Stracker finally had it out with him and said, *"Look, if you want that show, you go somewhere else and find somebody to pay you for it. I hired you to be in THIS show!"* And it didn't help that there were some nervous types from the network hanging around who agreed with him. For the first two years, until the ratings went through the roof, they just kept circling Jerry and tried to force him into making the show *Bonanza*. He didn't need some old guy in front of camera making the struggle more difficult.

CLIFF ADAMS: About the one thing I really do remember is that nobody had any respect for all my decades in the business. When I came up, no script was ever really final. The actors were able to adjust the dialogue to fit their own interpretation of the character, and that guy, Stracker, treated his words like they were, I don't know, Shakespeare. Not a word could be changed.

JERRY STRACKER: He said that? Bullshit. Lots of the actors improvised great bits on the show. They just didn't betray the show. He objected to a moment when the sheriff was permitted to freeze up with fear, saying that the hero isn't supposed to do that. I told him he was playing a protagonist, not a hero, and he asked me if that was one of those fancy-pants New York words. (*pause*) I guess I just outed him as bigot.

BUDDY SAMS: He basically confirmed everything anybody ever warned me about old white guys. Didn't like having a black man play his deputy. Said that weren't black lawmen at that time. I showed him a book about Bass Reeves. You know, that guy was the basis of The Lone Ranger. I was the one who talked Jerry into giving Reeves a cameo.

JERRY STRACKER: He spoke the lines, though. And eventually gave a great performance. I'll give him that. He acted the hell out of the part. He was gold on screen. Which meant . . . I would be stuck with him for the series. But I could have made that work.

CLIFF ADAMS: I didn't want the series. Not if they were going to keep that supernatural hugger-mugger.

ARLENE MOLINEAUX: If he'd done the show I would have walked. I would have had to. There were . . . backstage behaviors. The kind of thing people talk about a lot more, today. Back then, if a woman wanted a career, she didn't talk about that kind of thing. Poor Honey Pendrake ("Jeannie Armbruster," Seasons 1-5) and I used to regale each other with stories about our narrow escapes from that guy.

CLIFF ADAMS: She's lying. And dragging in Honey Pendrake, who isn't alive and able to testify, that's dirty pool.

ARLENE MOLINEAUX: The network wanted him.

JERRY STRACKER: I was faced with a serious problem. My lead actress wanted to go, my second male lead wanted to go, Adams would only take the show if I was forced to go. He would have installed some empty chair as showrunner and it would have been two seasons of *Perfect Old Sheriff*, every problem resolved with a gunfight in act four. I thought it was going to be one of TV's many abortions.

ARLENE MOLINEAUX: Then he dropped out, and I don't think he ever worked again.

CLIFF ADAMS: I guess they all think they got lucky, considering how popular the next guy was. (*shrugs*) It was between doing the show and fighting the cancer, and it turns out I had to fight the cancer longer than the show even ran. When I lost the leg, it was the end of the line for me. I did some gigs as narrator, and some audiobook narrations, but pretty much, I was done. Shame, though. What the show could have been, if they'd only listened to me.

Cliff Adams was interviewed three weeks before his fatal accidental overdose.

The First Season

Struggles with the network were not over, but with the pilot in hand, Stracker was able to get one of the actors on his original wish list for the character: grizzled veteran Mack Fortis, who, aside from bringing his own unique perspective to the role, was able to provide a smooth transition to his own characterization. Fortis, still a busy player in his late eighties, remembers fondly.

MACK FORTIS ("Sheriff Horace T. Booker," Seasons 1-6): When I found out I'd be replacing Cliff Adams, I almost turned the role down. I thought I was being hired for the wrong reason.

JERRY STRACKER: There is a very slight resemblance that could fool you in a dark room. It was helpful when we had to decide whether to retain the pilot. But there's absolutely no doubt that he made the role his, and more importantly, he got the feel we were going for. Even his prison record was a plus: he carried himself, on screen, like a man who had known violence, and could dispense it when necessary. But on set, he was a consummate professional.

MACK FORTIS: I don't shit where I eat.

ARLENE MOLINEAUX: He left us girls alone.

MACK FORTIS: I was half in love with a couple of 'em, but I don't shit where I eat.

WALLACE STEIN ("Doc Ferringer," Seasons 1-5): The man understood that the sheriff was supposed to be almost as chilling, every time he had to prove how deadly he was, as even the most murderous bad guy—a killer constantly in danger of going over the line.

CORLISS HANSEN ("Hogarth Malloy"): I hadn't ever seen him in anything else, and if I don't get in trouble for saying it, still haven't. You would think that by now I would have run into some old appearance of his, and I from time to time look up his IMDB listing to make sure I'm not going crazy, but I've never heard of any of that stuff, or anything he's done since. But he was fuckin' amazing to work with. Nasty old Hogarth would show up every five episodes or so, just to look sinister, and in half of them I had to go nose-to-nose with Mack, and I've got to tell you, whenever he told me I was on his list, I almost lost my water. He was scary. Barely human, it felt like. I always wondered why they didn't just cast him in my part, when he was that good at being bad; but the answer's that he'd turn around in the more peaceful scenes and be one charming son of a bitch.

WALLACE STEIN: Let me tell you something about Mack. We had this network liaison. I won't say his name because I have nothing good to say about him, but he was one member of what Jerry called the "Mundane Mob," the group dedicated to eliminating every element that made the show unique. When he saw the script for, what was the episode's name, the one about the lone rider who could point his finger at people and make them fall down dead—

JERRY STRACKER: "The Hand of Death."

WALLACE STEIN: Yeah, that one, the one that really got us noticed, and people on the street have been shooting me with index finger-pistols ever since. Anyway, this guy said we couldn't do that, because it was too violent. Imagine, a show where people shoot each other with real guns every day, and he thought pointing a finger was too violent! Anyway, that guy insisted on this script being shelved, and it seemed that Jerry had used up all his leverage for that particular season, because it was, even if that meant shuffling the arc stuff around. But the fight over this particular episode went on until the guy's backyard deck collapsed, right over the canyon it overlooked, killing him and two of his children. Mack had been as mad at him as anybody, but he spoke at the guy's funeral and it was like they'd been best friends for life. Not a dry eye in the house.

MACK FORTISS: Yeah, people actually mourned that piece of crap.

JERRY STRACKER: We ended up dedicating the episode to the guy. I guess you could see that as a nasty little in-joke, but we didn't see it that way. I mean, it was just a creative disagreement. We would have worked it out.

Season Two
Rotten Little Town ended season one with only mediocre ratings and ended that run on the cancellation bubble. Everybody thought the show was doomed, but then it received a last-minute reprieve, and the cast, some of whom had already gone on to other things, were called back.

JERRY STRACKER: The network would just plug in another show in the *Special Investigation Unit* franchise, which was already in the top twenty with the versions that ran on Tuesday and Thursday. I said to them, "Why not just do one every night of the week? Then you won't ever have to run any show that's even the slightest bit different!" But they had a good thing going, and knew it, and so it looked like our little show would just have to make way for another spin-off, *Special Investigations Unit: Hawaii. . .*

INGRID WINER (Writer, Seasons 1-4): Networks historically love setting shows in Hawaii. The weather's great, the scenery's terrific, and actors love getting cast in shows that are filmed there. Who doesn't want to be in the cast of a show set in Hawaii? The second they said the name of our replacement, I knew we were toast. But that was before Gerry Simpson got into trouble.

WALLACE STEIN: Second biggest Simpson scandal of the decade, folks.

INGRID WINER: Mr. "Track down and arrest the bastards" himself, the man who had made a fortune out of good cops punishing evil, having all that child porn in his home. Sounded like one of the villains on his show, saying he had no idea how it got there.

BUDDY SAMS: I hear he was passed around like a party favor in prison, and it couldn't have happened to a nicer piece of shit.

WALLACE STEIN: The point is that all of a sudden, the network had to fill that hour again!

JERRY STRACKER: The biggest problem was putting our cast back together. Mack had accepted a movie offer which would cut into our filming schedule, but getting him back in the fold was just a matter of changing the schedule, and filming our scenes three weeks in. Wallace hadn't hit the ground running and was still looking for work, so he was happy. Arlene had to fly back from London, where she was rehearsing for a show.

ARLENE MOLINEAUX: It was just one of those things. We were two days from our first tryouts when the producers suddenly soured on it. I didn't know why. All I knew was that it was my first stage role and that people said it would make me an A-list star, and that all this money was being spent on it, and that it all just popped and no one had any explanation. I was nearly out of my mind. But then the call from Jerry came in, that very same day. One door opens, another closes.

CORLISS HANSEN: I'd lost a big role myself, on *Life or Death*. Yeah, I would have been Dr. Benjamin Lancer, himself! I might have been where the guy who inherited the part is now, a fuckin' living legend! But in the early part of that summer, the railing on my front stairs came loose, and I spent the next couple of months in a cast. Was just coming out of the cast when Jerry called about the second season being a go, so in I was.

BUDDY SAMS: It was one of those cases like *Casablanca* where everything went right, and all these people who never expected much went into season two, thinking that we'd just signed on for no more than another year of a show that would limp along for another twenty-two episodes and then get forgotten forever. (*pause*). We didn't know that Jerry had an ace up his sleeve.

JERRY STRACKER: I knew that if the show was to find its audience, I needed a star to pull them in, if only for one season. And I got one.

The Coming of Tom De Lance

Generally, stars as big as Tom De Lance do not do episodic television until their careers begin to slip. By and large they don't even look at the scripts. But in late 1994, Tom De Lance was coming off his second Best Actor win and enjoying the box office lead of his latest film, Troublemaker, which would go on to spawn four sequels. He got to make them, but first he surprised everybody by agreeing to

join the second season of Rotten Little Town in second lead. We met up with him on the set of his latest blockbuster, Savage Eyes, set for release this November.

TOM DE LANCE ("Marshall Jack Hardeman," Season 2): What did they say in *The Godfather?* They gave me an offer I could not refuse.

JERRY STRACKER: It was a case of building the character for him.

TOM DE LANCE: It was a good character, a compelling, conflicted lawman who would gradually give into darkness over the course of the season. But there were a good dozen veteran players, and God alone knows how many unknowns who could have acted the hell out of that role. And going back to television at that point of my career felt a lot like retreating. Jerry just . . . .(long pause) explained to me why I should do it.

JERRY STRACKER: I just told him that if he played this part it would be one of his most beloved roles for all time.

TOM DE LANCE: He said that? Okay, let's go with that.

JERRY STRACKER: Just the announcement itself gave us a huge ratings boost. In terms of the story, it was helpful to create an upstanding, admired leader of men at the center of everything, who would seem to be the main character . . . and then to have him falter, and betray everything, and fail, and die at Hogarth Malloy's hands.

ARLENE MOLINEAUX: By the end of that season, everybody at home wanted to see Sheriff Booker nail that murderous son of a bitch.

BUDDY SAMS: We got tons of angry letters. Nobody really thought Jack Hardeman would die. They always thought he would pull off a brilliant escape at the last minute. But then came the finale, and wow. He was like the Ned Stark of our generation.

TOM DE LANCE: Everybody keeps saying that I gave the performance of my career. Maybe I did. I know that I don't see it. I try not to look at those old episodes, and I certainly don't go to any of the god-damned conventions, but I do run into scenes from the show from time to time, and what I see is not an actor giving a performance, but a man under tremendous stress barely holding himself together. They didn't need special lighting for the sweat to pop. It was . . . well, not necessarily because of the work schedule alone, a tough year. Maybe the worst year of my life.

Is there a reason you didn't show up to collect your Emmy?

TOM DE LANCE: I didn't want the damn thing in my house.

Why?

TOM DE LANCE: (Long pause) It's been many years. Let's skip it.

BUDDY SAMS: Tom has a long history of being a dick to people who were on the show. People go up and say hi to him, he calls them names. I think he's just such a big marquee name, that he doesn't like to be reminded that he put his superstardom on hold for a year, just because some then-marginal TV show gave him a call. It doesn't seem to have hurt him long-term. And if nothing else, it got his daughter her first acting job!

JERRY STRACKER: I have nothing against the man. He helped turn us around in the ratings at a very difficult time in his life—we didn't know how difficult—and we both got what we wanted out of the association. As long as he doesn't tell any tales out of school, I won't either.

MACK FORTISS: Yeah, I know the whole story. But I don't think about it much.

Third Season: The Coming of Angelica Delacroix

ANGELICA DELACROIX ("Melinda Harker," seasons 3-7): Look, everybody knows what happened to me the year before I cast. I was snatched out of my home and locked in some maniac's basement room, and no, I don't understand what he was after. I was lucky he wasn't some killer or rapist; just a collector, I guess. I almost went insane. Then, I guess he thought better of it, because he doped me up and dropped me off at some emergency room. Some people still think I made the whole thing up as a publicity stunt, and I said, "Sure, you think that makes sense, you put your life and career on hold and go hide out for a year." I moved back in with my Dad and was about thirty seconds away from picking some dangerous narcotic to get addicted to. I certainly didn't know if I wanted to go back to acting, especially since I'd had plenty of time to think about why this was happening to me and I couldn't think of anything but being the daughter of a celebrity. Who wants an extra chance at fame when you've been through something like that? But if I didn't want to spend the rest of my life as a terrorized shut-in, I had to pick up the pieces, So I finally called my agent to tell her that I was ready to go back to work. That's when I found out that Jerry Stracker had been looking for me.

JERRY STRACKER: Back then, nobody knew about her ordeal. Tom had kept it a secret all that time. The story didn't come out until ten years later, when Angelica wrote her memoir. When I think about how stressed he'd been, on the set, and how he cut off connection with all of us after the season was done—well, it didn't make any sense at the time, but ever since then, I can think of nothing more horrifying than having to pretend everything was normal when some evil shit had gotten his paws on my child.

TOM DE LANCE: "Some evil shit" is about right.

JERRY STRACKER: And of course, the people responsible have never been caught and are supposed to be still at large. It's got to be terrible, knowing that they could decide to go after his daughter again, at any time, if it ever occurred to them that they wanted to. Even if he had a clue who they were, and identified them, he could never be certain that there weren't accomplices still out there, prepared for reprisals if the ringleaders got caught. I, personally, would never feel safe. The thing he needs to keep in mind is that he gave them whatever they wanted, and they lived up to their end of the bargain.

TOM DE LANCE: No, I'm not going to tell you what the ransom was.

JERRY STRACKER: I don't have any more of a clue than anyone else.

TOM DE LANCE: I don't think it will ever be over, not in this head, and not in my daughter's. (*pause*) When I heard that the show cast her as this new continuing character . . . (*trails off*)

Why did you hold up casting Melinda until Angelica became available?

JERRY STRACKER: She'd auditioned for the original pilot movie and I'd never forgotten her. I wrote the part for her. If I'd known what she was going through, I might have gone ahead and cast someone else, but I'm glad I waited.

TOM DE LANCE: It sure was lucky for him that he knew exactly how long to wait.

JERRY STRACKER: Tom's family now, and he still has a bug up his ass where I'm concerned.

ANGELICA DELACROIX: My father had always been support-ive of my career, and he certainly liked that I was putting myself back together after a year in captivity, but he and Jerry just never got along. At the time, I hated that he would even think of standing in my way!

TOM DE LANCE: She didn't talk to me for two years.

JERRY STRACKER: I finally found out that all this was going on and called him up. I said, look, everything between us aside, this was her shot, and he was wrong to try to interfere with it. But I wanted to fix our broken relationship and I said, look, if it'll smooth things over, I'll just kill her off.

TOM DE LANCE: He would have done it, too.

ANGELICA DELACROIX: First I'm hearing of that, and it doesn't make me happy with Jerry. I'm not some appendage of my father, who needs his permission for everything. I'm an actress in my own right. (*pause*). But of course, he probably just said it as a joke.

TOM DE LANCE: I would like to point out one thing to anybody who loves that damn show: even if you think it's good, it ain't exactly a laugh-riot. There are no jokes in it at all. That's because Jerry Stracker has no sense of humor at all. If there any jokes in any episode, they belong to Ingrid or one of the other writers.

ANGELICA DELACROIX: Melinda was, more than Jerry ever could have guessed, the right character for me to play at that point in time: a privileged, but broken woman, coming off a nightmarish past that had come very close to breaking her but had instead made her stronger . . . can you imagine what it was like for me, coming out of a year locked in a basement room without seeing the sun, to channel those experiences into something strong? I told Dad that the show had kept me from falling apart, and that the cast and crew had made it possible for me to trust people again. I told him that if he wanted us to have a relationship in the future, he should stop trying to disturb that. And then I told him, of course, that Jerry and I were having a baby.

JERRY STRACKER: (*smiling*) We weren't in love. We agreed on that. But it was a late night, on the set, and despite what they say about producers and actresses . . .

ANGELICA DELACROIX: (*laughing*) He was always worried about the way it looked! All those years before the Me Too movement! But it was mutual, believe me. I've got a damn fine husband now, my second, but I will say this about Jerry: he's always been a good father to Peter. Had him half the year. Made sure to send Dad pictures of the times they spend together. All those wilderness hikes, river expeditions, deep-sea fishing trips . . .

JERRY STRACKER: Including now. Because whenever he's home from college he works at my production company.

ANGELICA DELACROIX: You can't peel the two apart.

JERRY STRACKER: Peter is the light of my life.

ANGELICA DELACROIX: As for me, I know prospective parents shouldn't have babies as self-therapy, but for somebody who had been through all that horror, it was tremendously freeing to be able to look at such a trusting little face and say, "I will never allow any harm to come to you."

JERRY STRACKER: I'm sure Tom feels the same way.

TOM DE LANCE: (*long pause*) . . . someone once told me that when you have children, you've given hostages to fortune. (*another*) And that, I guess, has been the story of my life. Protecting my hostages.

Season Four: Corliss Hansen's Reign of Terror
With the cast all in place and the show now the top-ten hit it was always destined to be, Jerry Stracker saw that it was time for the main villain to show how dangerous he could be. Season Four therefore contained all the most frightening episodes, mostly written by Stracker: "Night in Desolation," "The Plains Ripper," and "Devil's Bargain." Ironically, it was Ingrid Winer's "Schoolteacher's Song" that ended up winning the Emmy.

BUDDY SAMS: Yeah, that was one ruthless-ass year, wasn't it? Just when you thought the show had gotten as dark as it was ever going to, the writers would come up with something even more evil for Hogarth Malloy to do!

CORLISS HANSEN: I more than once had to tell angry people in supermarkets that I was just an actor, and that when I went home at night my wife and kids were waiting. Believe me when I said I almost quit the show to spend more time with them.

ARLENE MOLINEAUX: It was a rough year for many of us. Buddy had some growing substance-abuse problems, Corliss had a scare involving his kids—they had really only gotten delayed on the way back from school, but it was quite a scare there for a few hours! Wally's pregnant wife had a bad fall and lost the baby . . . honestly, it wasn't easy to return our focus to the show, but Jerry kept us in line. And the scripts were better than ever!

INGRID WINER: At the time I wrote "Schoolteacher's Song," there hadn't been an important viewpoint character added to the show since season two. All the characters had been profoundly touched by the evils they dealt with every day, the threats they all lived under, and it occurred to me that it was time to remind the viewers just how sick, how abnormal all of this was. So I brought in this sweet young thing schoolteacher, who in short order witnessed just what hellish compromises all the characters had made, with their morality and their sanity, just to go on living in this town where they were all being manipulated by ruthless puppet masters. **(Pause)** Of course, my original ending had her get away intact.

CORLISS HANSEN: I have to tell you, the original act four just sat there like a dry turd. The girl just says, "I don't have to be part of all this evil, I can go anywhere." And she rides out on the noon stage and the big last scene is just all the characters kind of just standing there in the middle of the street talking about how she had been such a breath of fresh air and how strange it was that she decided to leave.

BUDDY SAMS: My pals who worked on various incarnations of Star Trek said that she sounds an awful lot like Ingrid's "Mary Sue," whatever that means.

INGRID WINER: The point of that original ending was that all the horror they had already experienced in their lives had twisted them so that they didn't know what an unbiased outsider would see.

JERRY STRACKER: It wasn't enough of a jolt for our show, not for that point in the run. I thought, just how scary can the town of Sawblade be, if a nice lady like that could just get a noon stage and go on to live an ordinary life somewhere else? So I changed the ending. Kind of completed Ingrid's metaphor.

CORLISS HANSEN: What happened in the version as aired is that she takes her leave at the end of the second act. The third act is all her arriving in her new home in San Francisco, getting a new job, meeting a new man who's crazy about her, and thinking herself fated for happiness. All the things you want to see for that character, right? But then she wakes up in the middle of the night, alone in her little apartment . . . and boom . . . Hogarth's there. Biggest shock-scare that season.

JERRY STRACKER: We did a special public screening with a Q & A, at UCLA. The audience shrieked.

CORLISS HANSEN: All these years later I can still remember what Hogarth says to her, almost word-for-word, probably the most chilling monologue anyone's ever given me. [In character] *You think you can walk away? You think you can set foot on my streets and still belong to yourself? I'll always be right behind you. Don't . . . ever . . . think you're safe.* Then she blinks and he's gone, and you have that heart-breaking scene where she says no to the nice guy who was ready to marry her. As well as the closing text establishing that she disappeared forever, only a week later.

INGRID WINER: As a woman, I didn't care much for that ending. It took away all her agency, told the audience that she was helpless against this stalker. But, no, it was Jerry's show. We had to adhere to his vision.

JERRY STRACKER: This is one of the unresolved disputes that happen between staff writers and showrunners. I should stress here that I thought she was one of our best writers, and that she provided the kernel for one of our best episodes, the main reason I gave her all the credit and didn't append my name, even though I wrote a little more than half of it. Worked out pretty well for her, too, considering that the Emmy's officially all hers.

Emmy nominations in the dramatic episode category went to three episodes of Rotten Little Town, including Stracker's "Night in Desolation" and "The Plains Ripper." Ingrid Winer went home with the statue. It was such a great lift to her career that she was immediately hired to run a show of her own, the comedy *Penny of Philadelphia*, which ran five seasons and eventually won her three more statues just like it.

INGRID WINER: Let's just say I remain grateful to Jerry, for everything he did for my career.

JERRY STRACKER: We were all absolutely delighted for her, and you know what? Our little dispute on that episode led to a great moment for the *Penny of Philadelphia* blooper reel. Midway through her second season, with that show in the top five, there was a scene in an episode where she was directing, where Penny's new boyfriend is supposed to surprise her at home with flowers and a wedding proposal. I arranged for something else to happen. Instead of the actor it should be, the one who comes through the door, all dressed up like Hogarth. And he walks right past the star of the show and goes nose to nose with Ingrid, and by this point she's absolutely frozen with shock, and he says the same thing he said in "Schoolteacher's Song": *You think you can walk away? You think you can set foot on my streets and still belong to yourself? I'll always be right behind you. Don't ever think you're safe.*

CORLISS HANSEN: (*laughing*) I gave it all the same intensity and I think I scared the ever-living shit out of her.

INGRID WINER: They did it to me once a season, throughout *Penny*'s run. After the second time, I said that a joke was a joke but it was disrupting my set. Jerry agreed that enough was enough, but then he had Corliss dress like a waiter at one of my favorite restaurants and do it again.

CORLISS HANSEN: The whole place cheered.

JERRY STRACKER: I'm proud of all the careers we started, all the lives we changed. I'd like all my people to know how truly loved they are.

Season Five: The Year of Crisis

In season five, the supernatural events surrounding Sawblade accelerated to a fever pitch, both on and off the screen. Buddy Sams, whose drinking problem complicated the shooting of many episodes in season four and led to a substantially reduced role for most of the season, hit rock bottom. Corliss Hansen began intensive therapy to counter nightmares about the bottomless evils of the character he played. The show became the target of concerned parents. Two cast

members died under horrifying circumstances and Angelica Delacroix became subject to panic attacks. Throughout, Jerry Stracker kept a tight hand on production.

JERRY STRACKER: Look, if you put it that way it sounds like I'm inhuman. But the thing is, the showrunner is the one guy on any production who never has a life. He's always shepherding the next script, keeping his eye on the next story, worried about making sure everybody shows up on time. I always found out all these personal crises after they already happened.

BUDDY SAMS: I have to tell you; I owe my life and sobriety to the man. I'd started hitting the hard stuff pretty much all the time, a couple of years before, and pretty much lost half the entire prior season to my alcoholism, and there came a day when I couldn't speak any of the lines with any degree of coherency, and he took the time out from everything else he had to do to say that he needed me at the top of my game. It wasn't as simple as all that; there came a time early on when I lost twenty-four hours to alcohol poisoning and woke up in the hospital, not knowing how I got there. They said Jerry was the one who brought me in, and he was the one who got me into a thirty-day program.

JERRY STRACKER: I'll only say that he called me at his darkest hour, and that I'll be honored and humbled by that decision for the rest of my life. It did mean that we had to call in a substitute for his role, for the first third of the season, but we kept the role open for him for when he could return. (*pause*) Of course, that substitute caused other problems. That substitute was one Byron Nessman, making his TV debut—and departure—in the role of Coleman Hayes.

MACK FORTIS: I know of a guy who back in the sixties starred in one of the biggest movies of its year, one still considered a classic fifty-plus years later, though I never could make head or tail of it. He could have been a star, I guess. Turns out he didn't give a hoot about money and was happy just to get his one or two TV shots a year, because the only thing he was interested in was surfing, and acting was just his way of paying for it. That's a true story. I always thought he was a silly ass, myself, and I've got to tell you, I never thought I'd meet a guy like him until Byron showed up.

WALLACE STEIN: He hit his marks and spoke his lines and didn't stink up the joint, but he was about as memorable as . . . (draws a blank) Thus proving my point.

ANGELICA DELACROIX: Honey loved him, unfortunately. They had a prior relationship, and only got closer to each other when they worked together. The two of them took to long hours in the trailer, emerging for their scenes in a cloud of pot smoke. She wanted him to take over from Buddy permanently, and it was probably her idea when the two of them marched into Jerry's office and started issuing ultimatums.

JERRY STRACKER: I never intended him to be anything other than a temporary fill-in, but then Honey said that she wouldn't continue unless we also replaced Buddy with him, permanently. Could not be done, not and maintain the integrity of the show. We had an arc involving Buddy's character, developed at great length and with substantial artistry over half a decade, and it was integral to the planned conclusion. We couldn't just dump that, and I said so. They both walked off the set. Extraordinarily unprofessional.

ARLENE MOLINEAUX: I told Honey that this was a good way to ruin her career, but she just laughed at me. Said that she had "the goods" on Jerry and that he wouldn't dare do anything. It sounded like she had really bought Byron's bullshit, completely. Clearly, she had nothing.

BUDDY SAMS: I'm telling you, had I known that Jerry was fighting so hard for me, I never would have betrayed him by drinking as hard as I did. It amazes me that he visited me while this was going on, looking like about a million shades of hell, and I remember what he said, word for word: "After what I'm going to have to do to keep you on the show, if you get out of here, and ever touch a drop again, for as long as you work for me, I will kill you." He went on at great length, coming up with terrible things he would do to me if I ever did this to myself again; things like taking me out to the desert, slicing my belly open and stringing my intestines up on Joshua Trees, so the coyotes could get me. It was all hyperbole, of course, but to me it really showed that he cared.

ARLENE MOLINEAUX: I don't know what he said to get Byron and Honey back for an episode—maybe offered them more money, maybe threatened a lawsuit, maybe cajoled them with lies about Buddy, maybe just debasing himself as no man should ever have to; he cared that much about the quality of the show—but they came back together, long enough to appear together in a story that culminated in the two of them being ambushed by Hogarth Malloy, and ended with the two of them trapped in a cave with Byron's character bleeding out and Honey's half-delirious from a rattler bite. I happened to see the original script that came after that, which really rescued them both in a brilliant way, but . . . as we all know, it didn't work out that way.

What happened, of course, was one of the most notorious Hollywood crime scenes of the 1990s. Both Byron Nessman and

Honey Pendrake, who were at that point both heavily involved with the then-rising California cult known as The Church of Malachi, were found murdered and mutilated in the home they shared, their walls spray-painted with mottos from the Church's apocalyptic teachings. The most horrifying crime since the Manson murders, it led to massive investigations of the Church and the ultimate imprisonment of its charismatic leader Malachi Stardust on charges of sex-trafficking. The murders themselves, generally believed to have been committed by the Church's followers, are still officially unsolved.

ARLENE MOLINEAUX: I was absolutely shattered. We all were. Between that and the harassment by parents groups who said that the show invited such atrocities with its subject matter, I had a total nervous collapse, and I don't think anybody else was far behind me. We were all thinking, that year, "maybe we *should* pack it in."

JERRY STRACKER: We stopped production for six weeks, out of sheer decency, but after about four of them I called everyone back together—and this included Buddy—and said, "Look, if you all decide to quit, I won't blame you. But you have to ask yourselves, do you want to surrender to the madness of some wild-eyed, charismatic demagogue? Or do you want to finish the story we set out to tell?" They all went away to talk it over and returned to report that they were with me for the duration. I'm proud to say that they all made the decision professionals should have made. We dedicated the rest of the season to them.

CORLISS HANSEN: There was, for about five minutes, a popular conspiracy theory that I killed them, which disturbed the hell out of me because I played the character who killed them on the show. I had to keep telling people that I'm just an actor and I wouldn't know how to begin doing any of the things that were done to them. I'm not that guy. Neither was Jerry, who was in London accepting a prize that week. And even if you buy the even greater idiocy that maybe Jerry arranged it for some reason—I'd have to ask you the same question the cops asked themselves: what do you think, really? That he had some convenient psychopathic murderer on speed dial?

MACK FORTIS: Hansen said what?

BUDDY SAMS: About all I can tell you is that when I got back, still shaky as hell from hitting rock bottom, the atmosphere there was not the same. There was a grim sense of purpose. The end was in sight and we couldn't just pack it in, not at that point, even if some of us wanted to. As far as I was concerned, this last season coming up was my redemption.

And I have got to tell you, Jerry really gave me a lot to do, as we got closer to the end! Won me an Emmy and saved my bacon in the industry!

JERRY STRACKER: I'm honestly not fond of talking about the adjustments that had to be made, in the last year and a half. I had to scrap an entire arc that was meant for Honey, and find another player to do what she would have done in the last season. It weakened the overall storyline, as a whole. But that's the kind of thing you have to do when you're writing a serial drama: you work with fallible human beings, and you adapt. At least her character didn't just disappear between one episode and the next, is all I can say. The last episode she appeared in, the last episode Byron appeared in, worked just fine to exit both. (*pause*) But it was a tragedy what happened to them. It really was.

TOM DE LANCE: I was gone from the show for years by then, even if my daughter's involvement meant that I had to carry it with me, to the present day. I have nothing to say. And this is the last time I will ever agree to be interviewed on the subject.

Season Six: The Last Act

By the mutual agreement of everyone involved, nobody really wanted to make another full season, and so Jerry Stracker agreed to compress the final arc into twelve episodes and a reunion movie. By general consensus he performed this miracle admirably, with fourteen hours of superb TV that hit all the closing beats and provided the perfect send-off for everyone involved. The season's sole new player was Bree Destin, replacing Honey Pendrake's general position in the storyline as Sawblade's newest resident, storekeeper Felicity St. John.

BREE DESTIN: ("Felicity St. John," season six): My only roles up to landing the gig were TV commercials, and so I arrived as a fresh-faced young thing, eager to make an impression and not step on any toes. I knew about the prior season's tragedy, of course—you could not avoid knowing about it—but I was unprepared for how brittle everyone was, how beaten-down they were, how much they kept everything between themselves. I might not have made it to a seventh season if there'd been one, but I hit my marks and said my lines and the least that could be said is that I didn't add to the show's long list of problems while I was there. It got me to my sitcom, at least, which is where I learned what it was like to be on a *happy* set, for once.

JERRY STRACKER: I'm aware that Bree feels that way, and if there's one thing about the entire series that I regret above all else, is that I wasn't a warmer boss to her while she was there. But her self-appraisal is if anything too harsh. She was terrific, she was amazing, and she was no problem at all, not from her first episode, to her last. I'm delighted by all the success she's had.

BREE DESTIN: I have to admit that before I even set foot on set, I did ask some past and present members of the cast and crew what to expect, and that, among others, Mr. De Lance was very helpful.

BUDDY SAMS: I must admit I barely remember her from that year. She kept her head down and did whatever was asked of her, however difficult. It certainly added to her reputation for professionalism, and I have no trouble understanding why her career rose faster than mine. I won an Emmy that last year, and I still had difficulty getting cast in things. More got around about my problems than I ever expected. Lots more. It didn't really start until I was actively looking for a new gig, which makes me wonder where it came from, but hey, I did make a comeback after a few bad years, so I can't complain.

JERRY STRACKER: I think it's fair to say that he had suffered enough.

ANGELICA DELACROIX: We all went through hell on the series, but let's be honest. Except for Buddy and Holly—"Buddy Holly," we called them when they were together—we all walked away from that show with more than we had when we walked in. Jerry became one of the leading show creators in the business, and Buddy and Mack and Arlene and Ingrid and Curtis all had one of the all-time best hours of television, ever, in their respective CVs. Even Dad, who didn't get along with Jerry, got a grandkid out of it!

MACK FORTIS: All I can tell you is that I have maintained a relationship with Jerry Stracker all these years, because he's a man who knows how to get things done. If he ever needs me for anything, he has my number.

JERRY STRACKER: He said that? I'm touched. Kind of reminds me that I should call him. In this business there's always need for a man with his talents.

INGRID WINER: What isn't always clear in this business is that the compromises we make, to tell the stories we want to tell, are sometimes harsh and sometimes capricious, but always worthwhile if what you come up with is extraordinary. I've been busy since *Rotten Little Town*, but I've never done anything that seized the public imagination the way Jerry's story did, or resonated in the years to come the way his vision did. I'm not always happy to admit it, but it was the best show I was ever part of.

CORLISS HANSEN: I agree. And I still have nightmares. People keep asking me to play more villains and murderers like Hogarth again, but as much as I miss the edge, I'm happier with the comedies. They're more "me."

ARLENE MOLINEAUX: He's called me for this new thing he has in development at Fox, this sort of grim apocalyptic post-Holocaust thing, and said that he really wants me in it. He says the script is top secret. I guess I'll have to see him. I know that whatever it is will be hell. But you don't say no to Jerry, not when he really believes in a project. It's a dark joke among those of us who made it out of *Rotten Little Town* that he could probably get even Byron and Holly back, if he really wanted to insist hard enough.

TOM DE LANCE: He probably could, and I'm not joking. Half of us think he has the right connections. No, I'm not telling you what I mean by that.

WALLACE STEIN: We were all a big family, really. Not always close, not always peaceful, but all forever linked by that show, by what happened on the screen and what happened behind the scenes. I could live to age 100 and it will still be the headline of my obituary. I will never not be the guy who played Doc Ferringer. It'll be on my tombstone. It's always in my rear-view mirror, and sometimes it feels like it's catching up.

INGRID WINER: Certainly no one ever lets me forget it. Least of all Jerry. Corliss ambushed me with that Hogarth gag for the twenty-fifth anniversary of the premiere. Years and years since the last time! I almost passed out. I think he'll still be doing it, that Jerry will still be involved with him doing it, even if I leave the business and move to a chicken farm in Nebraska. Even if I retire behind a barbed-wire fence. I sometimes think it'll be the last thing I see before I die. That's one definition of a family, I guess. No matter how old you get, they still have to let you back in, even if you're bad. And you will never get away. Even if you want to.

At press time, Jerry Stracker has announced the signing of a contract to produce a big screen, big budget Return to Rotten Little Town. He has been talking about the project for years, but has always said that it will never happen unless he can sign every actor still alive whose character was still alive. Given some of the things the cast endured during the original run, it's surprising to note that he got everybody, including—and this is a shocker—Tom De Lance, whose character Marshall Jack Hardeman died in season one.

TOM DE LANCE: Let's just say I had to.

ANGELICA DELACROIX: I'm just thrilled! Three generations of the family on one set!

PETER DELACROIX: It's my acting debut, playing the new Marshall in town, at the onset of the twentieth century. As soon as I was signed, I knew I had to be the one who dragged Grandpop into the fold. He's always been so supportive of me, and I've learned so much from him over the years that I knew I needed him there! Especially with me doing so many of my own stunts!

JERRY STRACKER: I never require actors to do their own stunts, but Peter has demonstrated his skills, and I have absolutely, totally assured Tom that his presence on set is the best possible way to ensure that nothing terrible happens.

TOM DE LANCE: If there's anything anyone who's ever worked with Jerry knows, it's that he is always true to his word.

THE OLD
HORROR WRITER

He's harder to find than most. I have the basis for comparison because I've gotten to all of them sooner or later, from the big names to the obscurities. There are some who give up so thoroughly, and disappear so completely, that it's as if they never existed at all. This guy's far from the worst.

He's an old man now, twenty years removed from his last novel and ten from his last short story; he's no longer a member of HWA or SFWA, and the agency that used to handle his interests now has him in their estate file, sending out occasional contracts and two-digit checks whenever some foreign-language magazine situated in one of the new countries deigns to ask permission for, let alone, compensate, a reprint. Out of curiosity I made myself a voice on the phone and had to stay on the line with them for ten minutes before the receptionist was able to connect me with the member of the agency who knew who he was. The address they had was a post office box, and they hadn't mailed anything there for three years. I linger in the post office lobby for a few days waiting to see if he ever shows up, but he never does; I suspect he's paid for years in advance and forgotten that the address even exists.

Fortunately, I have other methods, and I soon appear in front of his home, which is not so much a home as the place where he wound up. It's a decaying little house in a decaying little neighborhood, a place of boarded-up windows and rusting automobiles, with a front walk stained by brown patches left by years of fallen leaves that were allowed to rot wherever they landed. The sky is gray, the air oppressive, in the way it's pretty much been everywhere, the last couple of decades. Before I get to the door, I hear the TV playing something with a theremin score, and wonder whether it's *Forbidden Planet* or one of its many imitators, before I knock and hear the old man grunt as he gets up from his chair. It takes him a long time to get to the door.

He is a pale and bloodless thing, an old man of the sort who used to be fat but lost most of that as age and infirmity sucked away his substance. He is bald, even on the sides, the skin over his ears tending to gray in the places where blood vessels near the surface have not rendered it pale blue. His teeth are yellow, his lower lip a permanent, and now drooping, pout. But his eyes are a rich brown that suggests depth. "Hello?"

I know the answer before I ask the question, but some formalities need to be respected. He confirms that he is indeed the old horror writer, though he's astonished that anybody remembers work that is now yellowing in magazines and anthologies that went out of print long ago.

When I tell him that it's his work that brings me here, he hesitates, casts a wistful glance over his shoulder at the music of weird doings on alien worlds, and lets me in.

The old horror writer is not a talented housekeeper. The floor has been swept just often enough to keep the place minimally presentable, but not enough to render it more than dingy. Books, pulled from one shelf or another and then put down whenever it occurred to him that he was done, sit on every flat surface. The house doesn't stink of cat the way some I've visited have, but a wisp of shed hair dances in his slipstream as he stops at the large but quaint TV, turns it off, and leads me further into the room beyond, which appears to be the most writerly of his three rooms. It is the room where the bookcases are all monuments to himself: his novels, several copies of each, his short story collections, many more copies of each, and, in one high place, a highly sought-after and well-respected trophy that would be shiny if he bothered to dust it. There is no desk, just a soft easy chair, and across from it a much-patched leather desk chair on casters. He gestures toward the desk chair, which I take, and asks if I would like something to drink; water, perhaps.

I say yes to water. He comes back with a tall plastic cup, and ice.

I note that it doesn't look like he writes here.

Yellow teeth flash. "I don't."

I ask if he's still producing.

"I tinker once in a while. I haven't finished anything in a little bit, but I tinker; there's an epic novel that tortured me for almost a decade, in the nineties, that I finally gave up on to save my sanity, that I still add a page to, once in a while. At this rate, I'll be finished with it when I'm two hundred and fifty years old. I suspect I'll be dead before I even finish another chapter."

Is he blocked?

"I've always been blocked. I was blocked when I started. That's the nature of the game. There were always stories I started but couldn't finish; novels I got eighty percent done but then wandered away from, like faithful wives I left in the lurch to pursue another that wagged her finger at me from the other end of the bar. If I could go back and finish all my fragments, without adding a single new idea to the pile, I'd be a wealthy man. If there were any place that would pay me for them."

There are still magazines, I say. Websites.

"Yes. Too many pay with love, or an insulting pittance not much better than love. Every once in a while I hear from one that still believes I'll have an orgasm over a penny a word. Did you know that was considered the low end of the pay scale a century ago, now? It was a scandal twenty years later, an insult twenty years after that, robbery when I sold my first couple of stories; now, with pecans going for a dollar apiece and oranges something only the wealthy can afford, it's a quarter dropped in a beggar's tin cup. Once I loved the art so much I was willing to take it. Then it became impossible to sell a story for even those poverty wages without somebody, somewhere, giving it away for free on line. Now I'm at the end of my life and I find my dignity's worth more."

But the stories, I say. I name a few of his that made a splash, a small splash, in the day. We talk a little about the one that inverted the vampire trope, where the predator was actually a volume of sentient blood, that invaded and possessed one victim's body after another; the one about the passenger plane that crashes in the afterlife; the paradise that erupts in horrific bloodshed every seven days; the siblings forced into gladiatorial combat; the professional torturer tasked by his king to find and render real that much-discussed and never-defined abstraction, the fate worse than death. I speak of the most memorable deaths in his work, like the woman turned inside out, or the art collector sucked into one of his more severe landscapes.

His tired eyes come to life whenever he discusses these masterworks and others, but after a while he seems to realize what he's doing and rejects it. "The problem is, that all of that was just comforting nonsense;

it mocked the genuine horror we live with by turning that emotion into a parlor game, making it an exercise in producing a frisson, rather than diagnosing the true evils that are out there. We wrote about zombies overrunning the Earth when the sad truth was that we were creating a terrible future of rising shorelines and endless drought and turf wars fought over glacial runoff. After my wife died, I had to move out of Florida; I became a climate refugee for two years. Once I was at a food bank and saw a cop beat some poor kid's brains out, for asking what line he was supposed to stand in. I'm not saying that I stopped writing about zombies and vampires that day. But it sure as hell seemed a lot stupider after that."

He's mentioned his wife, so I ask him about her.

His eyes go distant. "Do I have to talk about her?"

I ask him if he please would.

"She was the best part of me. And the worst."

How, I ask, was she was the worst?

"Between the two of us, somebody had to do the hard work of living. I was no damned good at it, so it fell to her. I was the dreamer. She was the doer. She went out and came back and had to listen to me saying I'd done another chapter, written another story. Then every once in a while a three-figure check would come in and she'd make me feel like a hero for a day or so. She was gone for a bunch of years before I accepted what I knew only vaguely when she was around—that to her, for all the love she showed me, I was like a pet dog, praised all out of proportion for performing the only trick he knew. You don't love that dog less because there's another you could have gotten, that knows every trick in the catalogue. You love it just as much, but make that one trick seem like it's worth more. I discovered how much effort that must have been, after she was gone and the praise stopped. I spend much of my time, these days, dwelling on just how much it must have cost her."

What would you tell her, I ask, if she could be returned to you for five minutes?

"That I never deserved her. That she shed light on a soul that had precious little of it. That I wish I had been a better horse for her to back. That I'm sorry I betrayed her by not being as remarkable as man as she should have had. That there was more wonder in one of her smiles than in any fantasy I ever produced."

I quote things critics said about his work; list the foreign languages it was translated into; catalogue the award nominations. I name the celebrated figures, some titanic, who attributed to him a number of synonyms for genius.

He listens and gives me a sad smile. "I used to cling to those. A writer's ego can be a fragile one."

There are photos around the room of him at one party or another, with famous figures of his era. Two or three are notorious for having had their fictions turned into movies or TV series, manna from heaven that the old horror writer has never had the good fortune to enjoy for his work. A couple of others in the photographs wrote terrific books whose influence is visible in the old horror writer's prose. I direct the conversation toward these mementos and he brightens a little, telling me about the aphorisms spoken by one, the character-defining moments lived by another. A few icons he won't talk about: the ones he says ended badly, or ended their friendship with him badly.

He falls silent a little after that. The old house settles and we listen to the sound it makes, like scared mice afraid that it might fall in on them. Cat eyes appear in a narrow crevice between stacks of yellowing books, blink at me, and disappear. The old horror writer was known for his cats, once upon a time; he used to include them as family members, in the bio blurbs at the back of his books.

I ask him why he's no longer writing.

He sighs. "Look. I don't know if I can explain it any better than this. There was a news story yesterday. Worldwide, zoos have agreed to stop breeding their tigers. They're the only place where there are any tigers anymore, but their stock is becoming so inbred that they judged it cruel to continue to continue to try to save the species. They long ago stopped replacing their elephants, because they realized that elephants went half-psychotic in zoos. Soon they'll be gone, the way the killer whales are gone, the way the bluefin tuna are gone, the way that wild tigers are gone. There are a couple of countries in Africa and Asia killing men and putting their wives and daughters into rape camps, a dozen major cities being abandoned all over the world, because they're no longer livable. There's a new disease, caused by heavy metals in the environment, affecting some of our more polluted countries: the occasional baby being born without brains.

"I could go on forever.

"The horror is out there without me writing it, and the sick thing about me after a lifetime of making things up is that I experience it not just as an appalled human being—though I am—but as a lover of the imagination, watching our possibilities contract to zero even as we continue to deny that it's happening.

"This is the damage a lifetime of nurturing that kind of imagination has done to me. I'm not so much disappointed that this world's turned to shit as by the awareness that we won't get to have adventures on another one. I'm not so much terrified that we've turned the Amazon into a parking lot, as by the suspicion that we've seen our last epic quest into unmapped places. I'm not so driven to despair by the evidence of so many human monsters, multiplying around us even as we breathe, but by the knowledge that we've catalogued everything that lives and that we know that there are no monsters of the sort that thrilled me as a child. In short, what I hate myself for, but have to acknowledge, is that I'm not as bothered by the sad wreck we've made of this existence, as I am by the destruction we've done to the world of make-believe.

"I've had to realize that horror fiction, bloody and disturbing as it often was, was not a way to engage with the awful, as to escape it. For me, a junkie breaking in and cutting my throat for whatever small amount of cash I've got lying around is just the sordid box known as real life; but a mysterious and shadowy thing, half-nightmare and half-man, drifting across a darkened bedroom in the middle of the night, with claw-like fingertips that become more like scythe blades the closer he approaches . . . that's *comforting*. It's reassurance that there's more around us than we can see, and that even if some of it is frightening, then at least it's proof there's more to the universe than what we see."

He shrugs. "I spent my life making up those stories, stories that *ended*, that left the readers licking their lips and saying to themselves, 'Well, that was a good one,' before they turned the page and moved on.

"And that, from the ridiculous perspective of ninety-five, turns out to have been a damned wasteful way to have spent my limited time on a dying planet."

The words dissipate in the dusty air before he registers that he's spoken them. He bites his lower lip, seems to register me as the stranger I am, and betrays a rush of shame that diminishes him in the few ways that age has not. "I'm sorry. I'm an old man."

"It's all right."

"I can't just blame being an old man. I've always talked too much. At conventions, I was notorious for it."

"I'm not upset."

"It's just that I know you came a long way . . ."

I say, "How do you know that?"

He opens his mouth, closes it. Tilts his head as the internal calculations play back as much as our conversation as he can remember. I see him register that he never actually asked me who I was or what I wanted, let alone where I came from. It always comes as a surprise. It is part of my glamor; whenever I am about, people sense the distance I have walked, and couple that to their own expectations. This man who has answered so many interview questions for so many fanzines, so many websites, so many author Q & A sessions and so many sparsely-attended bookstore autograph sessions, blinks as the illusion wavers and he catches the slightest glimpse of what I am and why I've come.

He says, "What are you?"

I flash fingers grown long and barbed, and festooned with hooks, and tell him that I'm whatever he wants me to be.

"I don't want you to be anything," he says. "I want you out of my house."

I could sever his head from his shoulders with a twitch, but I want understanding between us, and so I speak to him, in a thousand voices.

I tell him, with all due deference, that this visit is a gesture of love.

I explain that it's as he's said: so many of the deaths available to him, all jostling at the threshold known as blind chance for the opportunity to take him out at the end of his days, are too sad and mundane for one who has imagined such otherworldly sights and visions. In the next year, I explain, one of several things must and will happen to him. He might succumb peacefully in his sleep, but go undiscovered for weeks until his body has bloated and burst and sprouted life of its own; he might fall from a stroke, and find his limbs uncooperative as the telephone capable of summoning help sits untouched in plain sight; he might sense a certain pain linger in his belly until it metastasizes to his bone marrow and his brain, leaving him delirious in agony with no company but the hospice nurses who will see him as nothing more than just another anonymous old man; or he might suffer a day and a half of brutal torment at the hands of neighborhood morons who have talked themselves into the belief that he's a miser hoarding an immense fortune, and be left bleeding out as they flee upon deciding that he never had anything to offer them. All of these things already want to happen; they are merely racing toward him at approximately equal speeds, the winner a decision to be made by nothing more than random fate.

The splendid death I offer, the shapes I can assume, the sight of something alien and otherworldly that I can offer him, just because my claws slash, is just as horrid, in its own way. But it will also validate his lifetime of work, providing the epilogue to the single-author collection he's always been.

More, I say: the carnage I leave will render his death notorious. In the same way the sordid murders of one Wisconsin half-wit captured the collective imagination of so many fright merchants and made *Psycho*, *The Texas Chainsaw Massacre* and *The Silence of the Lambs* possible, his will become a perennial mystery, echoing down through just as many generations. Books will be written about what happened to him. Movies will be made about what happened to him. His story will be altered and amplified and told over campfires, for decades.

And then there's this, I say.

(By now, I have swelled to encompass the entire room, my scaly wings scraping the ceiling, my fiery breath making his many shelves of contributor copies smolder from heat that is more than normal combustion. I have assumed a form that would drive most men mad, and done so knowing that he will not go mad, not in any way that he has not always been; where others would shriek, he merely winces, taking me in, nodding as if his darkest muses have been confirmed. It is one of many reasons why I and all who come from the realm I call home, have always looked upon him and his ilk with such shining love; why we have visited so many, in their final years, and made offers like this to so many of them.)

I tell him that his own work will come back into print, worldwide, and he will at last achieve the true lasting fame that has always been denied him; that it will stay in print, for as long as frightening stories are told; that it will be studied, and admired, and copied, and above all, *read*, forevermore.

All he has to do, I say, is accept this fate, instead of the mundane ones that await, following months that have no compensating joys to offer him.

The choice is his.

He sits in his chair and blinks at me for so long that I fear he's gone simple from fear. But then the corners of his lips twitch, and he massages his chin between thumb and forefinger, unable to hide a certain anger even in the presence of a creature capable of disemboweling him in an eye-blink.

He says, "Then you'll own it."

"Yes."

"You'll make it a source of power."

"Yes. But think of what you'll have."

The cat I spotted before leaves its place of concealment and races across the room to his side, claiming his ankles, purring its bliss even as it ignores me completely. He snaps his fingers and it hops up onto his lap, where it curls up, an ancient animal content in the lap of its ancient master. He pets it absently, and gazes on me with undisguised pity.

He says, "Do you know what happens to all scary monsters, eventually, when they don't possess control over their own stories?"

It is the one question I've hoped he wouldn't ask, because it means that he knows the answer.

"They become jokes. Women fainted at the sight of Boris Karloff as the Frankenstein monster. Two decades later the character was a foil for Lou Costello. Dracula was once considered so ghastly that some parties thought the Bram Stoker novel unfit for civilized consumption. A century later, a puppet dressed up like him taught basic counting skills to preschoolers. I remember when a sparkly version of him romanced a wan teenage girl named after the Hungarian actor most famous for playing that most legendary predator on screen.

"Once upon a time, they made people scream. In short order, they all became themes for sugary breakfast cereals.

"The more popular the imagined nightmare, the sooner all the attention reduces it to impotent shtick—and if I can take anything from your visit, it's the awareness that perhaps this means my life's work had purpose, after all. It seems that I've done my small part to cast a light that keeps you, and all your kind, away from us."

I say, "You'll die forgotten. Your stories forgotten."

"Maybe," he says. "And maybe that means I'm irrelevant, that I've sucked as much fright out of what I've written as I'll ever be able to. That means you're irrelevant. And I want you the hell out of my house."

In the quiet that follows, I find that I once again possess the shape and dimensions of an ordinary human being; one more shadowy and mysterious than the average, but by no means the sanity-disturbing image I was a few short seconds ago. It should be more than enough than I would need to throttle the old fool where he sits, but it would take effort, and even as I consider it, I find that my human arms have become leaden, my human sinews too deprived of will to do much more than lift them. Their substance has turned smoky, transparent; too insubstantial to cast a shadow. Perhaps I can still kill him, but almost certainly not in any manner that anyone will ever consider legendary, not in any way that will give me and my kind strength. It would be pointless.

He continues to watch me as I rise, mumble inadequate thanks for his time, and drift from the room, fading so quickly that by the time I leave, aware that he is even now conceiving a brand new story in the dusty spaces behind me, I don't need to open the front door in order to pass over his threshold. I head up the walk to the street and am passed by figures who are just as transparent, but growing more substantial as they head toward his front door: a beautiful young woman, a dark-eyed and purposeful man, a figure belonging to neither gender who is nevertheless made of the same stuff. They nod at me as they pass, cursing me with the knowledge that there will now be more stories, more wounds to worsen the hemorrhage of our power.

Someday I will appear before one who accepts the offer.

It just hasn't happened yet . . .

www.ingramcontent.com/pod-product-compliance
Lightning Source LLC
Chambersburg PA
CBHW051143020726
47501CB00005B/1647